THE LOST TWINS OF ZILONIA

Part 1

MARGARITA KOUZNETSOVA

The Lost Twins of Zilonia / Margarita Kouznetsova. — 1st ed.
ISBN 978-0-9964477-4-4
Editor: Rebecca Martinez

Table of Contents

Dedication

*To my dear husband, my loving son, and
my precious twin daughters.*

Part 1

HOME

"Ms. Solunksi? Are you okay? You left your door wide open." Jack heard Lisa's voice and turned to see only the ends of her long, blonde hair as she disappeared into their neighbor's house.

"We don't have time for this," he muttered, following her into the house. It was sweltering inside. The little hairs on the back of his neck stood up and a chill ran down his arms. He moved through the house, peeking into rooms looking for any sign of Lisa or Ms. Solunski but finding only dust-covered furniture. Standing in the middle of the living room, Jack heard Lisa gasp as an icy wind suddenly whipped through the house. All the window shutters slammed closed.

He ran toward the sound of her voice, through one doorway and then another, until a strange sight made him slam stock still.

Jack watched as Lisa stood mesmerized by a huge painting that hung from floor to ceiling on the wall of their neighbor's home. A castle surrounded by mountains rising high in the background and delicately painted in vivid colors adorned the canvas. Her eyes flicked across the image to where a crystal medallion in the form of a curled serpent and adorned with diamonds was depicted. Jack saw a sudden change come over his sister as she fixed her stare on the lifelike talisman.

Jack brushed the dark locks from his forehead, a distraction to keep the unsettled feeling in his stomach at bay. But it failed to shake the unease he felt, his blue-green eyes narrowing upon his sister. Frozen squarely in a doorway in old Ms. Solunski's house, he was helpless as Lisa reached out toward the image. With the touch of her fingertips a sinister aura flared from the serpent's eyes and enveloped her slender form.

"Lisa, don't!" his mind screamed, but the words themselves came out as a hoarse gasp, barely loud enough to reach her.

Lisa, the tip of her index finger touching the canvas, was levitated from the floor and held mid-air before the painting, the light surrounding her pulsating as if the jewel itself was one with her heart. Suddenly, Jack saw her whole body shudder and go still like a curtain after a passing breeze.

"No, Lisa! Stop!" he yelled, his voice finding purchase and his words roaring across the room. He knew she heard him, because her head turned in his direction. But what he saw in her eyes, the long lashes fluttering, was a wildness he didn't recognize. She was not the beloved eleven-year-old he teased and spoiled.

For a moment she released the medallion and raised her hand up, as if in a trance. The aura dulled and flickered. In a hollow voice that sounded like it was coming from the wood of the frame and not from her, Lisa beckoned Jack to her side. Her blonde hair falling about her face and her eyes a bright blue, she cooed, "Come see, Jack. It's the jewel in my dreams, the one from last night." She floated transfixed and alien before the painting, the joyful and spirited girl that Jack adored gone, and he was immobilized by a fear he couldn't identify.

When Jack made no move to join her, Lisa turned back and again reached out to the lifelike image. This time, as she covered it with her small hand, it seemed to take form and fill her palm. Twisting it, the jewel came free, and as it did, the painting sheared down the center and curled away toward the frame. But instead of a bare wall, a bright void appeared.

Out of nowhere, a gust of wind filled the house. It swept across the floor and raced around the walls, picking up and twirling Lisa like an autumn leaf as it drew her into the gaping maw where the painting once hung. Released from the light's hold, she let out a terrified scream.

"Help me! Jack!"

Lisa's screams and helpless flailing released Jack from his frozen state. Snapped back to reality, he threw his muscular frame headlong into the room, giving himself over to the same powerful force that held his sister.

As Lisa was vacuumed into the void, she manage to reach out and grasp the edge of the frame, clinging by her fingertips as her brother neared. Her voice drowned out by the spinning winds, she yelled, "Help, Jack!"

Fighting through the swirling force, his arms and shoulders working as hard as they could, Jack closed the distance between them. Just as his sister's fingers slipped from their hold, he grabbed at her shoulders and felt the strap of her backpack catch in his closed fist.

Concentrating on his tentative hold, brother and sister went tumbling through the gaping emptiness, the sound of rushing wind and the light, now blindingly bright, robbing them of their every sense. Jack dug his nails into his palm, fearing that if he lost his grip, his sister would be gone forever. Then with one desperate yank, he drew her to him, so close that he could feel her fluttering heart against the pounding in his own chest.

Just as Jack thought everything around him was lost, the light and the wind grew distant, and the overwhelming pull that hurtled them onward began to lessen. Locking his arms around his sister as best he could, he found no defense against the dark numbness spreading throughout his entire body, giving into it without choice.

Together they fell headfirst into the endless space and slipped away into the void.

MAGNIFICENT POWERS

Kace and Orion, sharing the same handsome confidence and dexterity with hand tools, swung their hammers, smoothly driving iron nail after iron nail to join the planks that would soon be the new storage shed beside the small house. The twins' home lay nestled snuggly in the hills of the Sheevali-occupied territory, the woods coming up practically to their back door.

"I don't know why you think you do more work around here than I do," grumbled Orion, picking up where their argument had left off. He was the slighter of the two twins, if only by a pinch. "I'm the one who's up before dawn to get breakfast on the table."

"That's because the apron brings out the blue in your eyes," teased Kace, adding before his brother could think of a witty comeback. "Besides, the last time I did it you complained about shells in the scrambled eggs." He flashed his twin a cheeky smile and went back to hammering.

For anyone else who knew him that boyish grin would have ended the argument there, but Orion, with the same sun-kissed skin and hay-colored curls, was immune to his brother's charms. Sucking on his teeth, he said, "It was more like eggs mixed in with the scrambled shells, you mean. Even Alexa was making faces."

Kace shrugged. "You know I'm more the outdoors huntsman-handyman type." He then turned to Orion and flexing his right biceps, the hammer held high, said, "Come now, you wouldn't want this chiseled physique to go to waste in front of a stove, would you?"

What choice did Orion have but to laugh? Both boys were near identical as twins could be, taller and broader than most men and made rugged by the hard lands around them. "Okay, you win for now," he said, "but don't blame me if you find something wiggling about in your stew bowl come supper."

As the boys worked, their little sister, Alexa, was up on the front porch playing with her cat, Eldora, and enjoying the warmth of the late morning sun. For a moment they paused from their task marveling at the way its golden rays set her dark red hair shimmering vibrantly, her emerald green eyes a-sparkle, and the freckles scattered across the bridge of her little pointy nose to bouncing. Not yet twelve years old, she looked more each day like the woman she would surely become.

The peace of the moment, however, was rudely broken— Kace and Orion spotting a billowing dust cloud rising up from the road which lay beyond their property. Horsemen were fast approaching.

"Feels like trouble." Orion pushed his brother at the elbow.

With but a moment to spare, Kace spun away from his work, hissing a command at Alexa. "Get inside and don't come out. No matter what happens!"

Alexa darted off of the porch with Eldora and hid inside the house.

When the horsemen arrived, the boys knew them to be soldiers from the Sheevali Kingdom. Instinctively, each dropped his hammer and took up a more appropriate weapon. Kace grabbed a long handled shovel and Orion a toothy rake. They waited, muscles tense and at the ready.

A short, chubby man with a big black bird on his shoulder dismounted and approached the boys followed by a handful of his soldiers. He looked them up and down as if evaluating cattle, then asked, "How old are you two?"

Kace and Orion had heard officers from the Sheevali Kingdom of Darkness were going about the countryside conscripting local men as soldiers. They gazed steadily at the squat man before them, seeing his oily black hair slicked back and hanging down to his shoulders where the long, grey cloak of the Sheevali Kingdom was clasped to his uniform.

"Sixteen," Kace lied, clutching his hand ever tighter on the shovel, knowing that he and Orion had turned eighteen only a few months past. They had no intention of joining the Sheevali Kingdom's army.

One of the soldiers stepped forward and bowed his head close to the man's ear. "Captain Orlando, should we take them?"

The officer squinted and turned up one side of his mouth. Speaking to a soldier on his right he said, "Seems to me these boys are a tad too tall and their shoulders too wide for ones claiming to be so young. What do you think, soldier?"

The soldier said what was expected. "Not a day under eighteen, sir."

Orlando shook his head slowly and grinned. "Now, now, boys," he said, his tone sticky sweet, "Sixteen, you say? Do I look like a fool to you?" Then he snapped his fingers and barked the order to his troops, "Take them!"

The Sheevali men lunged at Kace and Orion, their dark cloaks ballooning out behind them, but both brothers dodged the oncoming soldiers easily, each delivering strategic blows with their toolshed weapons. With the danger before them, the twins forgot to mask their superior fighting skills—a strange talent for two boys from the hills. The captain would surely notice their training.

Orlando shouted out to four more of his men. "Apprehend these subordinates!" To the others he screeched, "Search the house! See what these boys have to hide. I want you to tear this place apart."

The brothers, leaping with the agility of mountain goats, avoided the attack and positioned themselves between the soldiers and their home.

"Don't come near or else we'll blow you away, you Sheevali cockroaches!" Kace shouted.

Afraid for their sister, Kace and Orion crossed their hands over their chests in unison and summoned up their inner force field, a strong surge of energy that cut the soldiers' pathway off and encased the twins safely behind an almost impenetrable curtain. A few of the soldiers ignored the young men and rushed toward the house where the front door was shut fast. The force field, completely invisible until the soldiers were upon it, suddenly sizzled with an electrical intensity that crackled and sparked through the air. The soldiers were thrown backward and to the ground, the house safe and sound.

The boys saw the look of disbelief on Orlando's face before his eyes flashed with rage, and their carelessness suddenly hit them with the full weight of its consequences.

Orlando yelled at his men, "It can't be! Only the Sheevali King and General Sebastian have such abilities. Everyone, Get back!" His face was shot red with anger and his teeth bared. "You want to play this game? Bring it on."

His men immediately cleared out of the way leaving a wide space around Orlando. The captain focused hard and brought his fingers up to his forehead. Bright sparks of electricity crackled in the air around him and emanated out into a focused beam.

"Burn the shed!" he screamed, and the beam shot across the yard.

An explosion rocked the valley, sending clouds of dust into the air. But as the dirt and debris settled, Orlando was shocked to see that the shield around the boys and their house held fast.

Shaking with fury, Orlando produced a small strip of paper and a pen. Paying no mind to the boys, he jotted a quick note. He then coaxed the black crow from his shoulder and fixed the note snuggly to its leg. Waving his pen angrily, he shouted, "To the Sheevali king, Ferocious. Go!"

In an instant, the bird darted away, leaving in its wake a solitary, inky-black feather which fluttered ominously to the ground in front of the twins.

The Lost Twins of Zilonia

HIDING

Jack and Lisa tumbled out of the sky as if from nowhere and crashed with a soft thud, a hillside of strange, sparkling flowers and springy green grass cushioning their landing. For a few moments both of them were afraid to move, Jack holding tight to Lisa, hoping that it was a bad dream. But when they opened their eyes they realized that their fear of being swallowed by the hole was true.

"We're alive," Jack sighed with relief. Seeing the petrified look on Lisa's face, he quickly pulled himself together, and being the big brother he was—his stomach churning—he put on a brave face of his own.

Jack helped Lisa to sit up and they sat in silence for a few minutes taking in their surroundings. He placed a protective arm around her. It was impossible to deny the beauty of the place, and they marveled at the light-purple colored skies and the melody of birds chirping from everywhere as if welcoming them to this strange, yet beautiful place. The sparkling blossoms waved back and forth with a gentle rhythm and the air was warm around them, enveloping them like a blanket.

Lisa let out a breath she didn't realize she was holding. "Where are we?"

"I'm not sure, but don't worry, sis," Jack comforted her. "We'll figure it out." He gave her hand a reassuring squeeze. He tried to sound positive but it was difficult when everywhere around them was so different to anything he had seen before.

Then without warning an explosion shook away the silence. Its noise deafening and unsettling, it echoed all about them, sending them cowering low into the long grass, Jack throwing his body protectively over Lisa. They lay there a moment waiting for the echoes to fade away.

Realizing that the sound had come from further down the hill, Jack told Lisa to stay put while he crept slowly forward to get a better look. Focusing on a small group of angry men charging toward a small house, he saw a sudden surge of electricity sizzle through the air and the men thrown backward.

"Lisa," he whispered, just loud enough for her to hear. "Maybe if we go down there, someone could tell us where we are and how to get back home."

Lisa looked frightened, "I don't know. They look kind of scary to me. Not that I can really tell from here, but they seem to be wearing uniforms like soldiers. I think they're fighting."

Jack crawled back to her. Then looking around, he saw a wide group of thick, squatty bushes between two big trees. It was the perfect place for Lisa to stay out of sight. He pointed to the hiding place. "Stay there and don't move! I'll be right back."

Tears welling in her eyes, Lisa clutched at Jack's arm and held him back. "Promise me you won't go near them unless you're absolutely sure that they're not dangerous."

Jack wrapped his arms around her in a reassuring embrace. "I promise, but I have to get up closer. What if somebody inside needs help? Who knows, maybe they'll be able to help us as well."

Lisa relaxed her grip reluctantly and dropped her head. "You'll do what you want."

Jack nodded solemnly and gave her a quick squeeze. Then he left Lisa to look on worriedly and wonder if everything would be all right as he ran down the hill.

Having made it without being seen to the cover of the forest that rose up behind the house, Jack saw a carefully stacked pile of firewood near the small cottage. Seeing his chance, he darted up and behind it, staying low and out of sight. From his new position, he noticed right away that the soldiers were up to no good, trying with all their wiles to gain access to the house. Seeing too that they couldn't get around the glowing light, he left the safety of his hiding place, and scooted closer until he could see into a back window. Peeking through, he spotted hiding in the corner of the room a little girl dressed in simple clothing.

The girl was clutching at a black cat, its ears and head all white. With each thundering blow by the soldiers against the force field she shuddered, muffled shrieks escaping her lips. Jack called out to her in a loud whisper, trying to attract her attention. At last she gazed up at him, the look of a caged animal in her eyes.

The girl's fear, however, quickly gave way to curiosity as her attention was drawn to Jack's appearance. Unlike the king's soldiers, he wore a chunky sweater with blue ripped pants, and his hair was cut in a different style.

Jack, from outside the window, saw her lips move. "Who are you?" she seemed to ask.

Just then, the cat jumped out of her arms and ran toward the window. Leaping upon a small table with a basin, the cat pushed the window pane with her paws, opening it just enough to escape; out she came and ran right into Jack's arms.

Alexa hesitated but a moment listening for her brothers, but then she too followed. Grabbing a plain scarf that lay curled up beside her, she slid across the floor and climbed up on that same table, the basin skittering off to one side. Alexa pushed the window open wider and slipped through the gap feet first. No sooner had her feet touched the ground, the cat jumped from Jack's arms and ran off into the trees.

"Eldora! Wait!" Alexa cried as she ran. But the cat was gone.

Jack could hear the soldiers' footsteps as they began spreading out to look for a way around the force field.

"Who are you?" Alexa demanded, pulling on his sleeve to get his attention.

Jack placed a hand on her shoulder and began leading her away from the house. "No time for that now. The soldiers are coming. We need to get out of here quick—for your own safety!"

"I'm not going with you!" she cried, shoving his hand roughly away. "How do I know you're not just trying to trick me? You might be a soldier in disguise!"

He gave her a flabbergasted look. "Do I really look like one of those guys to you? You can take your chances with them if you want, but it doesn't look good."

Heavy boot steps sounded a short distance away. The soldiers were growing closer every moment.

"Either you trust me now or you regret it later," he said firmly. "It's safe up the hill. My sister is there waiting for me." Jack turned and moved back toward the hill, certain she would follow. At first he heard only the sounds of the soldiers moving behind them, but then the girl let out a frustrated sigh and ran after him.

"I don't know who you are or why you're here, but I guess there's no other choice. Lead the way," she groaned, eyeing Jack distrustfully as she followed him up into the hills.

Jack sighed. He wasn't sure why it had been so important to rescue her but there was something deep within him that made him glad he had done so.

ASTOUNDING NEWS

The black-feathered Ferocious swooped down toward the Sheevali Castle to deliver Orlando's note to the king. Tall, carefully sculpted and granite-like cold, the castle stood in quiet solitude, surrounded by a protective wall that could be seen from miles away. Ferocious flew directly to the Sheevali king's quarters, landing nearby and taking a moment to preen his feathers.

The king's stocky frame was poised before his weapons collection as he stood examining each tastefully decorated piece, admiring their balance and their extravagant gemstones and engravings, each detailing a significant victory. Then his eyes shifted to a small plain knife, the most precious item in his collection. It had been a gift on his tenth birthday from King Theodore. It had once belonged to his real father. He had been killed along with his mother, and Grinage left orphaned.

Deep in thought and stroking his short beard, his black eyes piercing and intelligent, his expression indecipherable, he did not at first notice the bird's intrusion. Ferocious perched himself on the arm of the king's throne and let out a shrill cry. Grinage patted his black feathered friend. "Ah, my favorite messenger. What do you have for me?" He reached for the note tied to the bird's leg, and Ferocious let out a satisfied squawk. Grinage unrolled the paper, his eyes narrowing while he read Orlando's message.

Majesty,

I've discovered two twin boys with force-field powers. My soldiers cannot overpower them, and they might be hiding something or someone in their house. I believe their powers will be a great asset to Your Majesty's army, but I would need reinforcements to capture them for the kingdom.

Signed,
Your Loyal Captain, Orlando

The king crumpled the letter and chuckled as he squinted in thought, the wrinkles on his brow furrowing with concentration. Such power had not been seen for many years; it was rare and only appeared within the kingdom's oldest families. A spark of recognition flared within his eyes while he considered the implications of Orlando's letter. Had he finally located the Zilonian twins, lost now for many years? Twin boys protecting twin sisters—was it possible? His heart started beating hard and his throat grew dry. So long he had been searching without even so much as a whispered hint as to their location. And if it were them, there would be other powers as well. He needed to see for himself.

Grinage had many powers that he copied from other Zilonian people, but he favored orbing above the rest. It allowed him to transport himself to any other location instantaneously. The king strode to the mirror and smiled at his reflection with satisfaction. He wore his immaculate white cloak with its silver lining, his shiny black tunic and matching pants. But best of all were the sapphire cufflinks without which he never dressed. The king closed his eyes and, crossing his hands behind his back, disappeared in a puff of smoke. In a flash he appeared before the house, stepped out of the smoke with equanimity, and revealed his grand figure to his men.

The men fell before Grinage's feet, and Orlando ran forward, bowing low. "Your Majesty! You honor us by coming here."

Grinage ignored Orlando's groveling posture and marched right up to the twins, thoroughly examining each of them. The force of his presence, coupled with the strain of maintaining hold of their shield, caused the boys to shake. The king's power flowed from him with undeniable force. Combined with the soldiers attacking again and again, it was almost too much.

Grinage moved to the edge of the field and stopped, his face stoic and without expression. "Stop this nonsense now, or I will stop it for you," he growled, his voice menacingly low.

"Not on your life! If you want to take us down, give us your best shot," Kace shouted, often a little too cocky for his own good. The boys together glared back at the king defiantly and held their ground. What could a single person do against the two of them together?

Grinage's amusement spread into a wicked grin. Either these boys were stupid, he thought, or they were protecting something especially precious. But he also saw that they were already weakening. Like flies they were to him, easily swatted away. He let escape a triumphant laugh. "Silly boys, you have no idea who you're dealing with."

With one wave of his arm, he threw down their force field. With his other hand he extended his fingers. Out flew lengths of rope with the heads and voracious appetites of leeches. Before the boys could react, the leeches had wrapped themselves about the twins hand and foot and were clinging tenaciously. There was no attacking the king.

Both brothers screamed at Grinage. "You scum! Don't touch us! Get away from our home!"

Grinage, amused by the brothers' fierceness, let out a low laugh and said, "My, my, such spirited fighters." Then paying them no further heed, he turned to his soldiers and barked, "Search the house."

After turning the place upside down, the Sheevali soldiers found nothing. Orlando threw himself before the king. "Nothing, Your Majesty, just old rags and poverty. But I swear they were hiding something dear to them inside, otherwise why would they object so fiercely?"

Orlando continued to mumble frightened excuses, but the sound of the man's blubbering only sharpened Grinage's rage. Furious that he'd come all this way with no results, he burst out at the captain with disdain. "You useless worm! How dare you interrupt me for nothing!"

The soldiers around them froze in wide-eyed fear, waiting for the king's anger to fall upon them all.

But instead, the king lifted his hand, pulling Orlando's flabby frame from the ground and high into the air. He twisted his finger in a spinning motion, twirling the poor man faster and faster until he was a blur to the eye. All of a sudden, Grinage ended Orlando's spinning and pulled him down to land heavily on the ground.

"Don't you ever bother me with this nonsense again! If you can't do your job, I will easily replace you—or worse. I'll set you spinning for eternity."

Orlando shook at the king's sneer and gulped, pushing his disheveled hair from his face with trembling fingers.

The king was disappointed. He had hoped for so much more—specifically two little girls, twin sisters. But, alas, his hopes had been dashed again. He studied the squirming brothers and considered their worth. They weren't powerful enough to be the brothers he was searching for. Still, Orlando had gotten one thing right. Their powers would be a valuable asset for his army of magic warriors.

He whipped his cape back behind his shoulders and signaled to Orlando. "Bring the brothers to my kingdom."

Kace took a deep breath, tightening his muscles and snapping some of the bindings around his torso, freeing his hands. He lunged for the shovel lying on the ground next to him and hurled it at Orlando's head to prevent the fat soldier from torching their home.

"You stupid brutes!"

A horrifying sound escaped Orion's lungs and he yelled without thinking, "Stop, you monsters! Our—"

But before Orion could expose that their little sister might still be inside, Grinage turned around and, with a shake of his finger, silenced the boys by redirecting the flying shovel toward their heads. He then shifted his gaze to the trembling soldiers and gave the order. "Burn everything."

With a puff of dark smoke, Grinage disappeared the same way he'd come.

DEAR STRANGER

The trek back up the hill seemed long and difficult but Jack and his newly rescued friend finally made it back up to the top where Lisa was anxiously waiting. The sun was now westering quickly, throwing long shadows across their path and the air grew cold as the sun slipped toward the mountains in the distance, the vibrant colors of the flowers and trees giving way to muted browns and grays.

The girl turned to look at her home; it was fully engulfed in flames. The sight filled her with misery. She dropped to her knees and wept, eventually growing quiet. She wiped her tear-stained cheeks and mumbled quietly, "They can't hear me. It's too far."

Jack glanced at Lisa. He had no idea what the new girl was talking about, but he hoped that his little sister would make her feel more at ease. It seemed they were all a little lost and held captive by their fears.

As if reading his mind, Lisa moved toward her, kneeling by her side and with a gentle voice, said, "I know it's not much reassurance, but at least you're safe now."

"I'll never be safe. My house is gone, and I have no place to go," the girl said quietly, her pretty features veiled in sadness.

"Please, don't look," Lisa encouraged. "There's nothing you can do now. Believe it or not, we know how you feel. Our home is out of reach too."

"I doubt that our feelings are the same," the girl said, her dismissiveness unintended.

Lisa took a bottle of water from her backpack and offered it to the girl, but the stranger only shook her head and pulled her scarf up around her face, only her green eyes, deep and vibrant, and long eye lashes remaining visible.

Lisa held out her hand. "Please, don't be scared. We're not your enemy. I guess I haven't introduced myself yet. I'm Lisa, and you already met my brother Jack."

The girl nervously pulled back, not letting Lisa touch her. Every muscle in her body tensed as if she intended to dart away at any moment.

Jack saw the look of mistrust in her eyes. "Please, don't run. We won't hurt you. I got you out of there, remember? If the soldiers find us, Lisa and I are in just as much trouble as you."

Lisa stepped in, "We're kind of in trouble ourselves. We're lost here, and we don't know where to go."

The girl, suspicion edging her tone, asked, "How did you know that I was inside the house? The soldiers didn't even know."

Hope flashed across Jack's face. "We didn't. We heard men shouting and saw a big blast. I was worried someone might've been hurt inside or might need help; but I didn't know—not for sure."

Lisa shot Jack a nervous look and wrung her hands. "I saw the two young men protecting the house. Are they your family?"

The girl paused for a moment before responding to Lisa's question. She wiped away the tears and sighed before looking away and relaxing her stance. "Yes, they're my brothers. But I suppose they're gone now."

Jack let his head droop. Regret tinged his voice. "I'm sorry. I wasn't much help for them."

"It's not your fault. Those vultures have been after us for a long time, and now they've finally succeeded."

Jack's brow raised in confusion. "What are you talking about?"

But the girl didn't answer. Instead she appeared to be battling herself, pacing back and forth, rubbing her shoulders. Over and over, she spoke to herself, saying, "My house is on fire, and I don't know what's going to happen to my brothers. Maybe I should go back..." Then she would shake her head and look defeated.

Jack interrupted her pacing by pointing in the direction of the burning house. "Look! They're taking your brothers." The soldiers had tied up the boys and had slung them across the backs of two separate horses.

The girl covered her mouth as she watched the retreating soldiers, her brothers in tow, disappearing down the road and into the distance.

The soldiers now out of sight, and with Jack shivering as the cold cut through his clothes in a way he knew the girls must be feeling too, he turned his efforts to more practical concerns. He said to the girls, "Since it looks like we're going to be here for a while—at least until we're sure those soldiers are long gone—we better make ourselves more comfortable." He then started to search the ground. He gathered and stacked some kindling. Then using two stones that he found, he struck them together to try to spark a fire, but did little more than knock some dirt loose.

The girl watched Jack's unproductive efforts curiously and then a sudden realization crossed her face.

"Let me do it." Before Jack could reply, she snapped her fingers and a swarm of tiny fireflies appeared out of nowhere, gathering together in a tight little circle. In the blink of an eye, the little bugs created a foamy-looking mass and ignited it with a sparkle.

"Lisa, watch out!" Jack shouted and leaped up to cover Lisa from the fire. But all Lisa did was stare in wide-eyed silence at the girl.

The girl, ignoring them both, blew gently on the fireball and let it float toward the branches that Jack had carefully placed together. The fireflies disappeared as quickly as they came, leaving a cozy fire in their wake.

"Holy moly, what just happened? Did you just do some sort of voodoo hoax?" asked Jack, his voice trembling with every word.

"Holy moly?" The girl saw the amusing look on Jack's face and said with a slightly surprised but reassuring voice, "I know a few magic tricks. Why're you so astonished? It's as if you've never seen magic before."

Lisa quietly replied. "Because we haven't. I know it sounds crazy, but we're not from this world."

"We got here by accident," Jack added with chagrin.

The girl looked at them with distrust and frowned. But then she sighed, "All right. You can call me Alexa. I guess I can decide what to believe after you tell me your story."

With the fire now burning brightly, they sat around its edge, warming their hands in silence before Jack cleared his throat and began to tell their story, hoping against hope that Alexa would know of some magic that would send them back.

BUILDING TRUST

They sat together within the glow of the fire, the darkness crowding in around them. Jack warmed his hands and recounted the events of how they found themselves in the field.

"We were supposed to be on our way to summer camp," he said, shooting Lisa a withering look. "But this one decided she just had to check on our neighbor, Ms. Solunski. When we went inside the old woman's house, it was the weirdest thing I'd ever seen. Don't you think it was odd, Lisa?"

Lisa nodded vigorously, saying, "Definitely bizzarro! The whole house had this eerie feeling and every wall was covered with intense paintings of castles and mountains and stuff. "

Alexa looked at them both. "Bizzarro? Summer camp?"

Jack shook his head. "I guess this might be harder than I thought. Lisa just means it was strange, and summer camp is umm...well, it doesn't really matter. We're just saying that everything that's happened to us has been weird. We fell through a painting, and before we knew it we ended up in this mysterious world with magic and sparkling flowers like we've never seen before."

Feeling a little more lighthearted with the fire around them, Lisa giggled. But then thinking of her elderly neighbor, her face shifted to concern. "I hope Ms. Solunski is OK though. She wasn't in the house, and it's like she's always there."

Jack nudged his sister's shoulder with his elbow. "Don't worry, Lisa. That old bat will live forever. Death himself wouldn't dare go up on that porch."

Lisa admonished him with a pout, saying, "I don't know why you don't like her. She's such a nice old lady. Mom and Dad think so, too."

"Come on," he said. "You can't tell me she's not weird. It's like she's always staring at me as if she has something to say." Then thinking of his parents, he said, "I hope we can get back before Mom and Dad really start to worry. I told Mom on the phone that we were on the bus. Now we're stuck here and they don't have a clue."

Tears welled up in Lisa's eyes. "It's all my fault, Jack. I can't imagine how worried they will be when they find out about us disappearing without a trace," she said sobbing. "I miss them. I just wanted to check on Ms. Solunski."

Jack reached over and gently rubbed his sister's back. "I know. It's all good. We'll figure out a way back home, I promise. And then everything will be alright."

Alexa was sitting quietly, watching and listening and trying to find even a single thing not to trust. Intuition about people came natural to her and more times than not she could tell if someone was lying. Jack's earnestness convinced her that he was telling the truth, and there was something in Lisa's blue eyes—made ever darker by the firelight—that tugged lightly, but ever so persistently at the corners of her mind, as if she was supposed to remember something. And though she thought it some trick of the light, the girl, more than a little, shared facial features similar to those of Orion and Kace.

Lisa took sandwiches out of her backpack and shared them with Alexa and Jack. Alexa graciously took a bite, but she couldn't bring herself to eat much more.

"Thank you, but I'm not hungry anymore. Your food is unusual, but it's tasty." She handed the sandwich back to Lisa with trembling hands.

For a while, the three sat in silence staring into the dancing flames. Finally, Jack, licking the last remaining crumbs of his sandwich from his finger tips and washing it all down with a sip of water from the bottle they shared, said, "It's late, and I know that I for one am tired all the way down to my bones, so I can only imagine that the two of you are also. You should try to get some sleep. I'll stay up a while to keep an eye on things. Come morning, we'll all have a brighter and more cheerful outlook on things."

Lisa, wishing to see Alexa smile, added, "Since we're in a world full of magic, maybe something wonderful and unexpected will bring your brothers right back to you."

Alexa did manage to smile a little but then shook her head, saying, "If only things were that easy. But I do feel better that you and Jack are here with me."

Jack saw that Alexa was still shaking and tried to reassure her, "You know, we may not have magical powers like you but, if you would like, we'd be happy to help you find your brothers."

He looked to Lisa for support.

"Yes, we'd love to. Maybe together we could figure out our way back home. With your magic, there's got to be a way to get Jack and me back."

"I think with three of us, we have a better chance to help each other," Alexa said with gratitude.

They curled up near to the fire, Alexa and Lisa closing their eyes while Jack sat back against a great tree listening to the strange noises in the inky blackness around them and staring up at the stars. He didn't want to admit how scared he was to the girls, but fear had wrapped itself around him like a cloak. What if, he thought, there was no way to get back home...ever.

BROTHERS' INGENUITY

Kace and Orion came to, finding themselves tied up and draped over the saddles of two of the soldiers' horses. Their minds still hazy from the king's spell, each was trying to piece together what had happened. Close enough to speak to each other using silent communication, Kace, getting his brother's attention, said, "What happened to our force field?"

Given the rather awkward and uncomfortable position they were in, and the horses walking side by side, Orion could not see his brother—but, of course, he knew his voice. "It seems," he said, "the king simply waved it away. But maybe you were too busy at the time admiring your bulging biceps to notice."

Kace, glad that his brother still had his sense of humor, said, "I can't believe the dude is that powerful."

"Well, worse than that," said Orion, "we revealed our powers in a lost cause, giving the king a reason to be suspicious, and we don't know what happened to Alexa."

A silent moment passed between them, and then Kace said, his voice tinged with hope, "One thing we do know, is that Alexa wasn't in the house when the guards searched it and not in it when they set it on fire."

Orion, knowing there was no place she could have hidden within the house, it being so small and their beds separated one from the other only by hanging sheets, said, "For once her impetuousness may have done her some good."

Alexa, it seems, was very good at pretending to listen but then doing as she pleased anyway.

"I have no doubt," said Kace confidently, "that she got away."

"For once, muscle brain, I'm sure you got it right," agreed Orion, the tone of his voice lighter. "Which is all more of a reason why we have to get away from here and go find her."

Kace changed the subject, asking, "How far do you think we've come?"

Orion had no guess. "Why? Are you thinking about trying to reach out to her?"

"We can try," he said.

So they did, each of the twins focusing as best they could. But there was no response.

"She's probably too far away," suggested Orion.

"Or too busy to be listening," said Kace.

Still half a day's ride from the castle, Captain Orlando decided it would be best to camp for the night, not wanting his horses to take a misstep along the dark road and risk injury. The king was already less than content with him; he could only imagine the consequences if he were to return with a lame animal.

He signaled his men to dismount in a small clearing there alongside the road and ringed with tall, broad sugar maples. Even though the darkness was just starting to settle, fierce and curious animals could already be heard padding across the forest floor back in the shadows, snuffling through their great snouts and huffing with hunger.

Nervous and a little frightened, the soldiers gathered limbs and branches from beneath the closest trees and hastily made large watch fires, staying close together and keeping a wary eye to the woods.

Knowing that to arrive at the castle without the twins in tow would be disastrous, Captain Orlando took every precaution to make sure they could not escape. First he made sure that the ropes binding them foot and hand were quite secure and then he had both boys tied to a tree only but a short distance from the spot he had selected as his own. Finally, he assigned his very best man, Choonchu, to stand guard over them every waking minute. "Take your eyes off them but for a second," he threatened, "and I will make it my personal business to bring you most expeditiously before the king." Then before going about his business, he bent low toward the boys and using two long strips of fabric that he pulled out of his pocket he gagged them to prevent them from talking to each other. With his own voice carrying all the menace he could muster, he said, "Don't even think about doing anything funny." Again standing tall, he took two strides away, turned, and with two fingers he pointed to his own eyes and then back at the boys. "I'll be watching."

No sooner had the captain moved away, and with Choonchu standing there staring at them, Orion said, using silent communication, said, "We'll wait until they have all fallen asleep and then make our escape."

Kace's eyes looked up and down the hulking form of Choonchu, then he said, "What are we going to do about this big ox here?"

"Don't worry about it," said Orion. "Leave the thinking to me, biceps brain. For now, just pretend you're sleeping."

Kace was so tempted to come back with a crack of his own, but he decided it could wait. Instead, and following his brother's lead, he yawned as convincingly as he could with a gag in his mouth and let his eyes fall shut.

Late into the night, the fires having burned low and a chorus of loud snores rattling the leaves overhead, Kace reached out to his brother, saying "Are you awake, smart guy?"

"Who can sleep with all this snoring?" replied Orion.

"Uh, the guys snoring?" quipped Kace, settling the earlier score.

Orion let it go and instead said, "I think I have an idea."

"And what would that be?"

"Well," said Orion, "look up in that tree. You see that large seed pod just there almost above the ox's head?"

Kace saw it. "Yeah, what about it?"

"How much do you think that weighs?"

Not quite the same shape, but near the size of a small melon, Kace said, "Less than a pound I would think."

"Perhaps, but it must be as hard as a rock. I could make it bigger and heavy enough to crash it down. I bet it could send a man like Choonchu here nighty-night most instantaneously were it to somehow find itself hard down upon the top of his unsuspecting head. Then with that knife he has there at this belt, we could cut these bindings and be off into the dark woods before anyone would notice. I see one little problem though, he's a wee bit too far from the tree."

Kace could see the sense of it. "So what you're suggesting, if I have this right, is that were someone—like me, perhaps—to float the enlarged and very heavy seed pod from the branch where it currently hangs—once someone else makes it heavy enough to fall free of said branch—and to a place there above the ox's head where it can then be made to drop solidly upon said head, the resulting state of unconsciousness would allow someone skillful—that being me again—to transport the said knife here to where we are and using subtle movements free us that we may take our leave." He paused a moment to allow his brother to take it all in.

"Yes, that's what I'm suggesting. Can you do it?"

"Ready when you are. You start making it bigger, and as soon as it snaps from the branch, I'll stop it from falling, move it in position, and then let it go."

Concentrating on the task at hand, Orion went to work on the pod. Larger and larger it expanded, the branch holding it sagging more and more. Orion hadn't given that part of it much thought and worried for a moment that the branch would droop so much that Choonchu would be alerted.

Thankfully, Kace caught on and was able to intercede just at the moment that the pod fell free, at the time freezing the pod in place and keeping the branch from snapping back too noisily. "Phew," he said so only Orion could hear him.

"Good job, biceps boy. I'm impressed."

But Kace was too involved in the moment to respond. As quietly as he could, he floated the heavy pod right above Choonchu's head. Certain that he had it in the perfect spot, he let it drop in free-fall.

It may have been the sharp crack of the solid pod as it made contact with Choonchu's thick, bony skull, or it may have been the dull thump of the big guard's body contacting the ground—and the seedpod to follow. Regardless, Captain Orlando, sleeping but two strides away, momentarily lifted his head from the saddle he was using as a pillow, as if disturbed from his dreams, and seemed to look around. But no more than a second or two later, he placed it back where it was, shifted back and forth a bit to find the perfect position, and again was still.

Wasting no time, Kace focused his powers on sliding the long blade free from Choonchu's waistband. Smooth as butter it slipped free and, levitating inches off the ground, came effortlessly to within a hair from the bindings around Orion's wrists. Working only with his thoughts, he started moving it back and forth, the razor sharp blade cutting through the strong rope as if it were frilly lace. Orion's hands free, he grabbed the knife and cut the bindings around his ankles and then freed Kace.

Just then, the big guard moved his head and groaned.

Their limbs and extremities numb from lack of circulation, the boys struggled to their feet. Holding on to each other for support, they hobbled off into the darkness of the woods, the feeling slowly returning to their legs and arms.

"Keep going," said Kace. "We have to put some distance between us and this place before that big oaf wakes up."

Choonchu sat up and rubbed the huge bump on his head, totally clueless how he came to receive it. Suddenly, and to his great dismay, there in the pale glow of the dying fires, he realized his prisoners were gone. Sounding the alarm, and despite his splitting headache, he shouted, "Awake! Awake! The twins! They're gone! Everyone wake up!"

But it was too dark and no one knew which direction the boys had gone.

INTERTWINING CONNECTIONS

Jack awoke to the rising sun, his eyes opening to clouds stained like pink lemonade drifting high above the fields. Some looked like soft fluffy marshmallows, others like puff cotton candy, and some even resembling his mom's famed bloated cupcakes. Just thinking about those cupcakes made his stomach growl. He yawned. Even though at some point he had managed to fall asleep despite the strange noises of the night, it wasn't enough. He still felt tired. Reaching over, he tapped Lisa on the shoulder, waking her up. He hated to do it, but she had breakfast in her backpack, and anyway, they really should be getting their day started if they were going to find Alexa's brothers. "Come on, sleepy head," he said, his voice bright and cheery. "Rise and shine. Time to get up and have some breakfast." It wasn't going to be mom's cupcakes, but leftover sandwich sounded pretty good at the moment.

Alexa, sleeping just on the other side of Lisa, must have heard him too, because she rolled over with a tiny yawn, rubbed her eyes, and stretched her arms before sitting up. Turning toward Lisa, who was gradually waking up, she noticed strands of grass and leaves in Lisa's hair. Without thinking, she reached over to move the offending greenery. At her touch, a sensation—electrifying—leaped from one to the other, taking both girls by surprise and instantly surrounding them in an aura that seemed to be alive.

By instinct, Alexa pulled away. The aura blinked out and the sensation stopped.

Lisa, not quite knowing what had happened, turned to look at Alexa and their eyes met, neither one allowing themselves to breathe or blink.

Tentatively, Lisa leaned over toward her and said, "Do that again, touch my hair."

The expression on Alexa's face showed that she wasn't as eager to do so.

But Lisa only smiled. "Go ahead. It didn't hurt. I only want to see if it happens again."

Alexa cautiously raised her outstretched hand toward Lisa's golden hair, stopping only a finger's tip away. "It didn't hurt me, either," she said. "But it did tingle a little."

"Go on," said Lisa. "Don't be afraid."

Jack kept himself off to the side and chose only to watch.

Reaching out with her index finger, Alexa touched Lisa's hair with only the tip.

Just as before, a sudden glow of energy in the form of light closed around the girls like a big bubble, its edges wavering indistinctly.

"The heck—?! What in the world is going on here?" Jack muttered.

It was as if the two girls didn't hear him.

More forcefully this time, and trying to maintain some sense of humor, he said, "I'd feel better if the two of you would stop doing what it is you are doing there and put the light out. I know guys appreciate the ladies that have a bit of glow about them, but this is taking it just a little too far."

But the magical connection shared by the girls had them awash with such joy and intense familiarity that the world about them fell away as if nothing else existed but them.

Then quite unlooked for, there were voices coming from north of their position, but through the trees and not from the road.

Alexa, who only seconds before was lost in the moment with Lisa, dropped her hand and the bubble evaporated quicker than a candle flame before a sudden gust of wind.

The voices belonged to her brothers.

"Kace! Orion! I'm here!" she called out, momentarily forgetting all about Lisa and Jack and the strange happenings.

Kace and Orion hearing their sister's call, ran through the trees and burst into the small clearing, and noticing two strangers among them did what most big brothers would do. They placed their little sister to their backs and bowed out their chests.

"Who are you? And what do you want with our sister?" Orion snarled.

Kace, taking a closer look at what Jack and Lisa were wearing, elbowed his brother's side and said, "By the looks of those clothes, I'd say they're not from around here."

"You're not spies, are you?" asked Orion, his tone laced with suspicion.

Lisa had taken shelter behind Jack's back, but seeing and hearing the boys, she had the funniest feeling that she had seen them before, perhaps in a dream, or maybe even on television—but some place. She stepped away from Jack to get a better look.

When the twins saw her, they grew suddenly quiet. Then together, they took a step toward her as if drawn forward, but then stopped as one and stared.

Jack, misunderstanding their intention, took a step forward of his own, putting himself in their path and in front of his sister.

"Stay away from her!" he threatened, his fists balled up and held ready at his sides. "I'm pretty good with these."

Alexa, having grown impatient with the macho standoff, walked right between her brothers and around Jack and reached her hand out to Lisa.

Lisa took the outstretched hand in hers, and as before both were enveloped in the bubble of energy, its sunlight aura like a halo of soft rays beaming out from them in all directions.

Kace, his eyes fixed on the spectacle before him, whispered in his head so only his brother could hear him, "What do you think, Orion? It's some kind of trick? Some trick of Grinage? I don't trust them. I think they're trying to kidnap Alexa, get us all together. Some of the king's men have the power to change shape—or at least I've heard. We should just take them out before they get the chance to attack." He tensed himself, but otherwise didn't move.

Orion, ever the more contemplative of the two, said, using the same silent communication, "Let's not be hasty, brother. We may yet learn something useful."

Distracted by the voice of her brothers intruding on her thoughts, Alexa let free of Lisa's hand and turned to face them down. So that all could hear and in a tone that left no room for misinterpretation, she said, "You'll do no such thing. Jack saved me. He got me away from the house before the fire, before the guards saw me. He and Lisa agreed to come and help me find you two."

Jack, who of course could not communicate silently, was at a bit of a loss, having no idea what Alexa was talking about. Not the part about the house—he knew that part. But the 'you'll do no such thing' part.

That's when Lisa realized that she could do something her brother could not. Wondering only for a moment why she heard the twins talking when their lips weren't moving, and looking at Jack's reaction, well, she simply put two and two together. With Alexa still scolding her brothers, she leaned over toward hers and whispered, "Alexa and her brothers can communicate with each other without talking out loud."

Jack looked curiously at Lisa with his eyes narrow and his forehead furrowed, and said, "And how would you know that?"

She smiled at him in a way only she could, and said, "Because I can hear them."

As one, Alexa and the twins turned to look at her with stunned expressions on their faces as if they had all just been slapped.

Then, a big girlish grin spreading across her face, Alexa shouted, "You're my twin sister!"

Orion eyed Lisa and then Alexa, and then nodding his head toward his brother, his lips perfectly still, he said, "I suppose there is a bit of a resemblance."

"Poppycock," said Kace. "Let's test it out." He then said aloud to Lisa, and Jack too, for that matter, "If you can really hear us, what did I just say?"

Lisa only looked and shrugged.

"Just what I thought," started Kace, only to be interrupted by Lisa.

"Would that be the poppycock part or the test part?"

Kace frowned, "Ok, You can hear our thoughts, and you created a shield with Alexa. If you're really our sister, you'll have a power of your own. What else can you do?"

Fear entered Lisa's eyes. "I don't know what you're talking about. I can't do anything. No one has powers where I come from."

Kace softened his approach. "Have you ever had any strange feelings? Anything at all?"

Lisa shook her head. "No. I feel like everybody else."

"She can heal animals and people who are sick," Jack interjected. "People feel happier around her."

"Jack!" Lisa cried out.

"It's true. No sense in denying it now." Jack diverted his gaze from her, embarrassed.

Kace took out the knife that he'd taken from Choonchu and pressed the blade firmly against his palm, letting blood pool into his hand before holding it out for Lisa to inspect. Lisa saw his blood and was frightened. "I've never healed a bloody hand before. I've only helped birds and sick animals."

Kace moved toward her, still holding out his bleeding hand. "Just try."

Lisa didn't know what to do. She looked at Jack for reassurance and then shook her head in fright. Before Jack could say anything, Alexa cut in. "Leave her alone, Kace. No one's ever taught her. How could she know how to do it?" She smiled sweetly at Lisa and nodded toward Kace. "It's all right. Just concentrate and do your best."

Lisa nodded at Alexa and took Kace's wounded hand and placed her hands over it while closing her eyes in concentration.

Nothing happened. Lisa grunted in frustration and started pulling her hands away when Alexa stopped her with an encouraging smile. "Keep trying, I can feel you have it in you."

She gently took Lisa's other hand in hers and they both closed their eyes. Again Lisa had the same unbelievably calm feeling as the light again surrounded both girls. When Alexa let Lisa's hand go, the light disappeared, but Lisa still felt Alexa's energy coursing through her veins. Suddenly, the blood disappeared from Kace's palm and the wound completely healed. There was no doubt that Lisa was their lost sister. Everyone stood staring in silent shock.

Jack was the first one to speak. "This is too weird. Lisa, I think you just became a fairy."

"I feel.....a bit strange," she admitted. "I don't really know what's happening." Lisa turned to look at Alexa, then wide eyed at the boys. "How can I be your sister? I mean, I don't know you, any of you. I don't even live here. I come from a different world. And Jack is my brother."

Alexa placed her arms around Lisa and they shared the same crackle of energy. "You might not believe it yet, but you will. We are most certainly connected."

Lisa smiled at Alexa's obvious delight. "It may take some time..."

Alexa feigned sadness.

"Oh all right...sister." She laughed.

Alexa grabbed Lisa's hands and both girls swirled around laughing, creating a circle crackling with electricity.

"But what does it all mean?" Lisa interrupted. "Was it fate? Did you summon me?"

Kace and Orion shook their heads. They seemed concerned and it felt as if a shadow of fear was cast over them.

"What is it?" Jack asked stepping forward, "What are you not telling us?"

The twins gave Jack's hand a shake and forced the cloud of fear from their faces, "It's always nice to meet more family. Sorry we were tough on you."

Jack laughed warily, but let the moment pass. "No problem, I wasn't exactly nice myself. Now, can we discuss how Lisa and I got here?"

Kace shook his head in wonder.

"You might as well start from the very beginning,"

HOW IT ALL STARTED

I am the man and every girl is going to love me.

Lazy sunlight streamed into the room. Jack opened his eyes and smiled. School was finally over and summer break was here. He leapt out of bed and darted into the bathroom, barely containing his excitement for summer camp. Leaning in over the sink, he admired himself in the mirror, tweaking the earring in his left ear after it went awry in his sleep.

Over the past school year, Jack had transformed into more than a good-looking young man—he was a hunk. Making daily trips to the gym, he dedicated himself to building his strength and sculpting his physique. Now, as his almond-shaped eyes, sparkling green with flecks of blue around the iris, stared back at him in the glass, he saw that his hard work was paying off. Finely honed muscles complimented his high cheekbones, small, straight nose, mischievous smile with accentuating dimples and charmingly unkempt mop of jet-black hair. Tilting his head just right, he took another look at the stud in his ear and grinned. It gave him that subtle hint of danger every man should have.

At age seventeen, this was going to be the last summer of his youth and he was set for breathtaking adventure, or at the very least, a full-blown summer romance that he would recall with a smile in his old age. What girl in her right mind, he thought to himself, can resist a physique like this, especially attached to such a handsome face. And then he laughed and was glad no one was around to see the silliness.

There was, however, one catch complicating Jack's plans. His little sister Lisa was also attending camp this summer, and he was expected to play the big brother the entire time. But, smiling into the mirror, he had to admit, she always seemed to bring him good luck.

The truth is, Jack had an undeniable soft spot for his sister.

Almost twelve years-old and looking nothing like him, Lisa was a beauty with big, sky-blue eyes and long, sweeping lashes. Her blonde waves fell about her face and shoulders as soft and gentle as cascading water. Yet with all of the compliments that came her way, she remained polite and a little bit shy.

Although Jack played up his self-centered bravado around everyone else, his sister had a way of keeping him grounded. Because of that, he often went out of his way to surprise her with little gifts when he could and kept a protective eye on her always. Of course, it didn't hurt that this softer side of him made quite the impression on the girls around him too.

Leaving the bathroom, he went back into his room where he started going through his closet to prepare for the trip. Not wanting to bring along his whole wardrobe, he selected only the coolest styles he had, carefully folding them so they'd fit neatly in his knapsack. The last thing he included was his camera, which he wrapped carefully in a sweater.

When not in school or at the gym, Jack had worked all year doing odd jobs around the neighborhood and mowing lawns to earn enough money for his prized possession. When Lisa saw Jack's new toy, she absolutely loved it and pleaded with him to let her use it sometimes. Since it was nearly her birthday, he decided that he would make it a present after they settled into their cabins. The camera would make Lisa happy—and it would give her something to do at camp while she explored the wildlife and he checked out the locals.

Downstairs, their mom was already preparing the kids' favorite breakfast—hot pancakes. She set the steaming platter on the table with a bottle of maple syrup and called everyone to eat.

"Kids, come downstairs," she cried out. "The pancakes are getting cold."

Lisa ran down the stairs full of excitement and raring to go. Jack followed slowly giving everyone the opportunity to take notice of his precisely coordinated outfit, the chunky, dark-blue sweater fitting snuggly around his biceps, the ripped jeans and styled hair lending him an almost feral ease of motion.

Adriana moved on from breakfast and began making some sandwiches for the bus ride. Their father was reading the newspaper aloud. He liked everyone to know what was going on in their hometown.

"Huh, in a few weeks there's going to be a big car sale at that lot south of town. Says here that the prices are going to be unbeatable. Son, I think it might be time for you to upgrade your motorcycle to a car. What do you think, honey?" He looked at his wife.

Adriana's expression moved smoothly into a huge smile that showed off her white teeth. "I'm for it. You know how I feel about his bike. It may attract the girls, but it scares me out of my wits."

Jack shot a mischievous grin at his mom. "I think you might be right, Dad. I could fit way more girls in a car than on a motorcycle."

Adriana just shook her head in response. "I'm not even sure that I care how many girls you try to fit in a car, as long as you're safe out on the road."

Lisa leaned forward and peered at the paper in Jordan's hand. "What about the summer antique fair? Is there anything in the paper about that?"

"That's not until late summer. There won't be anything in the paper about it yet."

"So I won't miss it?" Lisa's blue eyes sparkled. "I want to see if I can find a medallion like the one I had a dream about last night. You should've seen it, Dad. It was so shiny and beautiful, and it made me feel...special somehow. Do you think I'll find it?"

Adriana joined in Lisa's enthusiasm. "I'm sure you'll find one. Remember when you found that nice bracelet last year?" Adriana motioned toward the delicate, beaded chain around Lisa's wrist with her spatula. "That was such an exquisite find, and you dreamt about that too. I think you might have a sixth sense about these things."

Lisa laughed and admired the sparkling bracelet. "It's true, it is quite fancy. Maybe I have a special power when it comes to spotting nice things."

Jordan looked back and forth between his wife and daughter, listening to them chat as if Lisa was already a grown woman. He had to admit that his little girl was growing up fast. "Don't worry. You'll be back before you know it. Camp is only for a couple of weeks."

Lisa sat up straight, puffing herself up to appear larger. "I'm not worried. Jack is coming with me. He'll take care of me."

"Will I?" Jack shoved the last bite of breakfast into his mouth and slung his bag over one shoulder. He shot Lisa a playful grin, and she gave him a mock pout in response. Unable to tease her any further, he went to her and gave her a big bear hug. "Of course I'll stay by you. And to prove it, I even have a surprise for you."

"What is it?" Lisa asked, her eyes widening with excitement.

"If I tell you now, it wouldn't be a surprise would it?" he said with a wink. "You have to at least wait until your birthday. It's just two weeks away. Or if you behave yourself I may give it to you even earlier."

Lisa had been talking about summer camp nonstop for weeks. She was excited about being out in nature without the conveniences of home for such a long period of time. Of course they had been camping before as a family, but this would be her first time without her parents and for more than just a couple of days. She felt nervous, though knowing Jack would be there gave her confidence.

The bus station was right across the street, right next to the high school. There were only a few houses between their home and the station, meaning they could wait until the last moment before heading out.

Jack adjusted his bag and smiled at Lisa. "Ready?"

Jack picked up Lisa's backpack and tested its weight. "I'll carry this, Lisa. It's too heavy for your scrawny arms."

Lisa patted the back of Jack's bag. "I only pack it this heavy so someone else will carry it. Looks like you're my latest victim!"

Adriana gave Jack both a hug and the sandwiches and then kissed Lisa on the forehead. "Have a safe trip, you two."

"And have fun!" Jordan added.

Down the walkway and out the gate, brother and sister made the turn as they did every day taking them past their neighbor's charming, little house. And as always, Lisa made ready to wave at Ms. Solunski, who was always sitting on the porch.

Ms. Solunski was a grumpy and unfriendly lady who didn't seem to like anybody. Her sour mood had chased all of the other neighbors away, but Lisa and Jack's family was always kind to her.

Lisa especially liked Ms. Solunski, but Jack treated her with a level of polite caution. Her presence sent shivers down his spine, and he thought her to be hiding something. What's more, she would stare at Jack as if she had something she wanted to ask, but then say nothing.

But this particular morning there was no one on the porch and the door appeared to be slightly open.

Lisa's face wrinkled with concern, and she said to Jack, "Something's not right. Ms. Solunski is always on the porch, and look, the door is open. Maybe we should check on her. Maybe she needs help."

Jack dismissed Lisa's concern with a wave of his hand. "Come on, we'll be late. She just went inside for a moment. She can't be out on her porch all the time."

Jack had almost managed to steer Lisa away when his phone rang.

"Are you two on the bus yet?"

"Uh, yeah, Mom. We're just sitting down. They got a nice bus this time. Super plush." Jack lied, trying not to worry her. He hated not telling her the truth.

"We'll see you when you get back. I just wanted to hear my kids' voices since you'll both be gone for two weeks away from cell reception. Tell Lisa I love her, and I love you."

"We're fine, Mom. I love you too. See you soon."

Jack hung up the phone and turned to find that Lisa wasn't anywhere in sight. Instead, Ms. Solunski's front door hung wide open.

Jack rushed into the house. "Where in the world are you, Lisa?"

THE KING'S RAGE

When Orlando arrived at the Sheevali Castle, he and his deputy Choonchu reported directly to the king to break the news of their captives. Orlando's words came out in a frightened mumble. "Your Majesty," he said, dropping down to one knee. "We took every precaution, but the boys are powerful. There was nothing we could do to prevent their escape."

Grinage, who was examining a map of the kingdom, looked over and glared most displeasingly at Orlando. "I did everything but wrap them in a bow for you, and now you have the audacity to come into my chamber and tell me you managed to lose them?"

An unintended laugh, high-pitched and nervous, slipped from the captain. "Everything possible was done, my Lord. They were tied hand and foot to a tree, the two together. I forbade them to speak, and my best man, Deputy Choonchu, was assigned to the watch."

Choonchu hearing his name knelt also.

"I don't care what precautions you took if they didn't work. All that matters to me is that you let them escape."

Cowering beneath the wrath of their king, both bowed their heads to the floor hoping for mercy.

Grinage bit his lip against his anger while he pondered the news of the boys' escape. Was it possible, he wondered, that they possessed powers hidden even from him? Forbidden to speak, yet...dare he think they had the means to communicate silently, mind to mind—as would the Zilonian twins? The very thought that he had half of the pair within his grasp and these bumbling idiots let them escape—well, that was just too much incompetence for one king to bear.

Without warning he whirled upon Orlando, his tone low and dangerous. "If you think this is a laughing matter, Captain, then I'll turn you into entertainment for the entire kingdom."

The king waved his hand and Orlando began to shrink in size and turn a bright red color. Wings formed on his tiny back and extra pairs of legs sprouted from his miniature torso. He had been transformed into a red shaking fly.

Laughing cruelly, the king crowed, "Let's see how funny it is when every person in the castle tries to squash you flat. I've even made it easier for them with your bright color. We will see if you get smarter." And then with a swat from his hand not meant to find its target, he shooed the buzzing captain away.

Choonchu, his eyes frozen to the floor, shook uncontrollably but he dared not move lest he call attention to himself.

But Grinage hadn't forgotten. "You are useless," he said and then orbed the trembling guard out the chamber window and left him floating over the garden of punishment.

54

The garden, enclosed by high walls, was a labyrinth of snaking paths and tangled hedges. Eerily formed fountains and trees and bushes trimmed into geometric shapes grew randomly here and there as if planted by a drunken gardener. As silent as stone, not a bird or an insect of the meanest sort would dare enter.

Choonchu, hanging helplessly, cried out to his king, "Please, my lord, have mercy on me! It wasn't my fault."

Grinage responded with but a cold stare. His lips straight and with the merest shrug of disinterest, he absently moved a single finger and let Choonchu drop to the ground. Most immediately, the soldier was sucked beneath the soil. And then, just as suddenly, in his place bright-blue cylinders sprouted up from the dirt. Each had the most wondrous shape of a crystal flute, the soft, sullen notes of its baby-blue water glistening forth, its voice joining the mute and eerie chorus of all the other fountains already there.

Grinage, who by then had floated into the garden to stand by his newest creation, peered down into the heart of the fountain and saw the tiny blue topaz forming at its base. If only for a moment, the Sheevali King allowed himself a smile—one more gemstone to add to his collection.

Back in his chambers, Grinage felt his spirits sink. If these were the boys he had been seeking for so long, they would know, he suspected, if their sisters were alive or not; and perhaps, where they might be.

For years he had been searching for them, sending his spies into every niche and corner of the kingdom. A few years past, identical twin boys—much easier to describe given their age—and a little girl—only an infant when the twins were sent into hiding—were reported seen with an older man in the streets just on the other side of the castle walls. But before he could set his men out after them, they walked into the darkness of the forest and were gone.

Every inch of those old trees were searched, and the valley below too, never finding a trace of the children he desired—just one old man living alone in a hunter's shack.

But this time, Grinage was even more determined, quite convinced that he had the boys he was after. And now that their house was burned down, they'd have nowhere to go but into the city. He would order his soldiers to comb every street and turn out every building. First the boys and then the sisters. Where one pair was, the other was sure to be near. He would have them and he knew exactly what he was going to do once he found them!

THE MYSTERIOUS BOX

Before leaving to find safety somewhere else, the kids decided to make one final trip to their house. There was something, said Kace and Orion, they had to recover from the rubble.

Standing before the charred husk in the cold morning light, Kace, Orion, and Alexa couldn't help but think of all they had lost—first Bruno and now the house itself.

After the Zilonia Kingdom lost the war to the Sheevali king, all of their family, including their parents, disappeared. Nobody knew what became of any of them, and it was safer to not stay in touch. Only their uncle Bruno stayed with the boys and Alexa.

Despite his long, silver hair and aged look, he'd retained an uncommonly youthful vigor. He cared for them and taught them how to care for themselves and for the house. He taught them about their family roots and about their lost sister, Lisa. Their uncle helped them recognize and understand their magical powers, how to develop and rely on them. He made sure that Kace, Orion, and Alexa knew how to advance and control their abilities. And he warned them of the dangers of the Sheevali Castle, where they would be hunted for their heritage. But his teaching turned into uncharacteristic silence whenever they asked about what happened to their parents or to the Zilonia Kingdom. He always found a reason to stop the conversation or simply changed the subject. It was too painful for him to speak of.

All of the kids became nostalgic when they entered into the ruins of what remained of the house.

Kace had a faint smile on his lips, remembering the time when they found this old cottage and made it their home. "I'll never forget when Alexa scared the wits out of all of us with those ghosts as we were fixing the roof. I almost fell off when I saw them surrounding her."

Alexa laughed, "Silly, they weren't ghosts, they were my fireflies. I just dressed them up a little."

Orion joined the conversation, "Maybe It was a game for you, but Bruno, Kace, and I almost had heart attacks. We thought you were being attacked."

Alexa turned to Lisa and rolled her eyes. "They're exaggerating. I just needed somebody to play with. I found a few old bed sheets and wanted to make something out of them. I saw before how Bruno snapped his fingers and I liked that gesture. That day I tried to imitate him, but instead of just a nice sound, a bunch of glowing insects appeared in front of me. Naturally, I covered them with the sheets."

Lisa's eyes grew big and questioning, "Naturally?? Weren't you scared when they appeared out of nowhere?"

Alexa puffed her chest out proudly, "Not really. It felt similar to when I touched you earlier today. I felt calm and composed. On the other hand, Bruno and my brothers were terrified. You should've seen their faces when they fell through the roof. It was such a mess!" she giggled.

Orion added with fondness, "Now that we think back on it, it was kind of funny, wasn't it? Bruno lifted one of the sheets and hundreds of sparkling fireflies surrounded Alexa. I remember Bruno shaking his head and saying they were Alexa's best friends. He also mentioned that we were lucky that she didn't summon the wasps or who knows what would have happened."

Jack's face had a wary look, "Wasps?"

Kace made a scary face, "They're another of Alexa's 'pets.' But those venomous creatures aren't nearly as nice as her little sparkly fellows."

Jack, who was listening intently, found himself oddly curious about Bruno. "What ever happened to your uncle?" he asked.

The siblings passed serious looks between them before looking back at Jack sadly.

Orion took the initiative and began to explain, "One day, Bruno left for the market in the city to buy some essential clothing and spices and didn't come back.

"From then on, our lives changed. We had to grow up immediately." Orion's voice cracked and his eyes began to well up from the painful memories.

Kace stepped in for his brother, "Bruno prepared us for the worst—he was always planning a few steps ahead. Before he disappeared he showed us where he'd hidden a metal box under a brick in the chimney. 'Only open this in an emergency. Otherwise, it's best not to think on this box,' he'd told us."

Kace walked over to the crumbling chimney and took the worn metal box from its hiding place. He then held it in his hands, feeling the loss of his uncle more now than ever before. He looked up at Orion and then at the gaping hole where their roof once was and let out a sad groan. He opened the box and motioned for Orion to join him.

Kace and Orion looked inside of the metal box and found a map, yellow with age, along with an object shaped like a leaf. The leaf was made of glittering crystal, dark-green in color and icy cold to the touch. There was an engraving in the middle but time made the words impossible to read.

Kace held up the objects for the others to see. "Now that we're all together, we're even more vulnerable. We have to find a safe place to hide." At his words, a blast of cold wind rocked through the dilapidated building, sending burgundy leaves spiraling in from the trees outside. Kace picked up a leaf and looked at it. "The weather's only going to get worse with the rains coming. We have to hurry and find a safe place soon."

"Rain?" Jack asked. "It's cold, but I don't see any rainclouds. How do you know it'll rain?"

"The leaves tell us," Orion explained. "The weather changes every day here. When they're green, the weather will be nice. Burgundy means heavy rain. You don't even want to know what black means. It's scary."

Kace continued, "Let's stay on the subject. If the Sheevali king finds out that we're reunited, he'll try to capture us and we'll never have a chance to find out what happened to our parents. Bruno's map has a note on the back. It says that if we're ever in trouble, we have to go find our aunt Greta. Try the Fairyton Institute in the city."

Kace and Orion hardly remembered their parents, let alone their aunt. The boys were very young when they last saw her at a family gathering. But they remembered the kindness in her voice as she tucked them into bed and read fairy tales to send them to sleep. At night they dreamed of the tale she told of two royal twin brothers and their twin sisters.

Their mother had just given birth to their sisters, Lisa and Alexa, and Greta told them that when they grew older, they would go to army school and their sisters would go to the Fairyton Institute, a school for ladies with special powers where she worked. There they would all perfect their magic skills.

Kace never understood why Aunt Greta would work at the school for girls when she was a royal who never needed to ask for anything. Their memories from the night at the gathering urged Kace and Orion to look for answers from their aunt. But first they needed to find her.

Everyone leaned in close to see the map that Kace held aloft. "There's an address here. Uncle Bruno told us to use it only if we have to. The map that Bruno hid gives us a place to start, but the city will be dangerous and we don't know for certain that Aunt Greta is still at the Fairyton Institute. The Sheevali king will stop at nothing to find us."

"We have to try," Orion added. "There's nothing left for us here anyway and we must hurry." He looked at the sky noticing that it wasn't light purple anymore; the clouds were forming a dark-gray mass. Kace brushed a hand through his hair. "Everyone keep an eye out. We'll split up so Orion and I together don't alert the soldiers."

The clouds gathered overhead, dimming the day's light to a twilight darkness. Looking through a gap in the wall, they could all see a storm swirling over the Sheevali castle.

"Bad magic." Orion warned. "We must all watch out."

LOOKING FOR GRETA

By the time the city lights came into view, the sun was already beginning to drop below the horizon and the dark clouds were sending plump drops of rain splashing to the ground. It was slow going through the city while the group moved about, trying not to be detected.

They had decided to split into two groups, separating the identical twins. Kace and Alexa went first. They were holding the map and trying to navigate through the city. Orion joined Jack and Lisa as they followed Kace and Alexa, keeping a safe distance from them, yet always in sight. Finally Kace and Alexa located the address that Bruno gave them. It was a tiny cottage nestled near a bustling café. They looked around to make sure the coast was clear and slipped inside the home.

Lisa, with Jack and Orion, was in the process of catching up to her siblings when she heard fast-approaching footsteps behind them.

"Stay where you are and turn around slowly." The voice was both powerful and intimidating.

Orion turned and glared at the two Sheevali soldiers who stood examining them, fists clenched in tight balls. "We're not going to give in without a fight," he whispered to Jack. He moved into an aggressive stance.

Jack stopped him, his hand on Orion's shoulder. "I've got this." Brushing his hair from his forehead, he addressed the soldiers, an innocent smile across his face. "How can we help you officers this cold evening?" he asked.

"Aren't you the helpful fellow?" The tallest officer said, pressing his face close to Jack's. "Not exactly the nicest evening for a stroll. Where are you headed?" He brought his torch up close to each of them studying their faces in the sputtering light.

Jack grinned and pointed vaguely in the direction they were going. "We're on the way to a party up the street. It's sort of a costume party."

The taller man gave their clothing a scrutinizing glance. Noting Jack and Lisa, especially, he said, "Granted, it's an odd get-up. But what's it supposed to be?"

"We're gypsies from the far lands of the south. Rather authentic, don't you agree?" Jack beamed. Of course, he had no idea if there even were gypsies or far lands to the south. But he doubted these two dodos did either.

"Maybe so," the tall guard said, "but your friend doesn't look like he has any costume at all."

Jack gave an exaggerated smirk in the direction of Orion. "Who? My mate, Toby here?" Jack said the first name that came to mind. "He's a bit of a stick in the mud." The tall guard only nodded. "Well then," Jack continued, confident he had pulled it off. "If it's OK with you we'd better get going. They won't let us in if we're late, and it's not getting any warmer out here. We wouldn't want to get locked out in the cold tonight."

The soldiers raised their torches once more. The tall one then grunted. "I guess you're not doing any harm. Get lost before we change our minds, and don't let us catch you out this late again. We have orders to stop anyone who looks suspicious."

"Well, good night, then," Jack said, and then without appearing too eager hustled the others along. "Come on guys." And off toward the cottage they went.

When the kids approached the house, Kace and Alexa, who were watching the scene from the window, had the door already open for them. They quickly looked around and darted within.

"What was that?!" Kace cried. "We were so scared when those soldiers stopped you. We thought they'd drag you away. How'd you get out of that?"

Orion exhaled with relief. "It was a close call, but Jack handled it like a pro!"

When the kids entered the old structure, they were pleasantly surprised. Outside, it looked like a rickety shack that hadn't been cared for in many years. But Inside was cozy. There was a red brick fireplace in the center of the main room, small but perfect for their little group, and two tiny bedrooms one to each side.

Before heading out again, Kace and Orion looked through the closets. There they found some coats, worn and faded but well-cared for. They put them on. As expected, each coat adjusted itself to fit Kace and Orion just right.

Lisa gasped at the sight. "Did I just see what I think I saw?"

Alexa laughed. "That's something else you'll have to get used to. All our clothing is made to one size. No matter how big or small, everything self-alters to fit the wearer." She slipped her foot out of one of her boots. "Here. Try mine on."

Lisa grabbed the boot and ran to sit near the fireplace where she could try it on. Alexa followed and they fell into chatter punctuated by giggles.

Orion paused at the door before departing. "Jack, keep the girls safe. We'll be back soon with some food."

"Are you sure you don't want me to join you? Those Sheevali jerks weren't joking when they said that next time they'd arrest us."

"We'll be fine. You gave me a good lesson on how to handle them," Orion said.

Once outside, the boys made their way toward the edge of the city to the school where they hoped Greta still worked. They held their coats tight and flipped up the hoods to keep out of the cold rain.

Staying to the shadows so as not to be spotted, they made their way cautiously through the streets. Before long, they came to a bridge spanning a deep ravine on the other side of which there was a beautiful mansion atop a hill. It was the Fairyton Institute—and a magnificent sight it was. The grounds were surrounded by a great wall, and there were stone-paved roads winding along its heights. The boys saw guards lighting lamps along the wall to keep watch over the school even in the darkness. There were other guards positioned along the bridge.

Kace and Orion searched for a way across but without success. Then suddenly, off to the side of the road, Orion spotted a black and white cat. It was Eldora. He'd know that cat anywhere. He nodded to Kace. They darted over toward her.

Bending down to pick up the cat, Orion said, "Eldora, what are you doing here? How did you find us?"

The cat made a satisfied trill and then jumped from Orion's arms, moving off a short distance and then stopping as if waiting for the boys to follow.

Kace slapped Orion along the shoulder and without saying anything ran after. Orion, a moment slow on the uptake, was soon but a stride behind. When they stopped, there where the base of the bridge ran down into the dark stone was a cleverly concealed opening. The cat had led them to a secret way beneath the bridge.

The secret way was a dark, narrow tunnel that ran beneath the bridge and at one time had served those who constructed it. It ran straight and true, bringing the brothers out into a small culvert, now dry, on the other side. With no trespassers expected on this side, their way to the front door was free of any obstacles or guards.

Orion hung back behind as Kace, rubbing his hands cold from the rain, rang the doorbell. After a moment's wait, a woman, small in stature and bent with age, opened the small window in the door and looked out at them.

Kace looked at her hopefully. "Hello, there. We're looking for Greta. It's very urgent. Could you please call her?"

The grouchy woman snarled at the boys. "There's no Greta here. Go away or I'll call the guards." The little window slammed shut, and the boys were left with opened mouths at her rudeness.

"It was nice talking to you too." Kace made a face. "Now what do we do?"

"Let's go." Orion suggested. "We can come back later. We can't go getting into any confrontations. It looks like it's going to be an exceptionally cold night, and on top of that we need to figure out what to put on the table tomorrow. Without money we'll starve."

REMEMBERING BRUNO

The boys, drenched from head to toe, returned to the cottage with nothing to show for their trouble. On top of that, the pantries were bare, leaving Kace and Orion feeling tired, wet, and hungry. Jack, though, remembering his mom's sandwiches, rummaged through his backpack and pulled out the last ones. It wasn't much, but there was more than a bite for everyone.

As the boys ate their share silently at the kitchen table, Lisa and Alexa—seated on the floor by the fire—couldn't get enough of each other. Just the slightest touch sent them into a fit of giggles they could hardly control. They made a game of grabbing each other's hand, sending them each time into delighted shrieks as the bright, electric magic sparked and popped around them. As they played, the sparse objects within the house vibrated and rattled, some even teetering and ready to fall, suggesting there was training and guidance yet to be had.

When Kace and Orion were learning their powers, they had Bruno there to help. But they had no idea how to address the gift shared by Alexa and Lisa. It was new to all of them and beyond their understanding. What was obvious, however, was that it was growing stronger by the minute.

Later that night and off to a corner of his own, Jack found himself pondering the rather odd chain of events of the last day or two. He thought of his parents back in their regular home on their regular street and wondered what part they might have in this crazy, magical world. And Lisa, his sister, were they even related? And if not—what connection remained to them, if any? Could it just be some coincidence that they'd spent their childhood together? Or did he too have a role in whatever was happening? He was certain there had to be a connection between them, something that two strangers could never have. He felt it. He knew it.

And there was that birthmark on the top of his right shoulder, the one shaped like a leaf. The one his friends swore was a tattoo. Then when Kace held up the crystal he pulled from the box hidden in rubble of the cottage, such butterflies in his stomach he had never felt before. The crystal was identical to the birthmark, right down to the size, shape and detail. He thought that it just had to mean something, but so far no special powers.

The night was growing late, but Jack wasn't tired, and neither, it seemed, were the girls. They were busy in their own little world. Kace and Orion, however, seated over at the table seemed particularly subdued. Moving over beside them, he said by way of conversation, "I can't do the things that you and the girls can, but I want to help. If you have a plan, let me in on it."

Orion, meeting his eyes, asked, "What do you remember about yourself and Lisa? Have there been any odd people just kind of popping up?"

Jack shrugged. "Only the old lady, Ms. Solunski. But she's just cranky."

Kace perked up at the name. "Isn't that the lady whose house you went into before you ended up here?"

"Yes," confirmed Jack but without seeing the connection.

"What's she like?" asked Kace.

It was Jack's turn to shrug. "She's very strange. She spends most of her time sitting on the porch watching everything in the neighborhood. But she's always friendly to our family—in her own way—though she never talks to anyone else. Most just stay away from her. Our parents make a big thing about us being respectful and that we always wave and say hello."

Kace gave Jack a suspicious look. "You don't think she's a spy, do you?"

"I doubt it," Jack laughed. "And if she is, she's pretty bad at it. All she does is sit on that porch and watch."

Orion looked at him quizzically. "Are you sure you're not like Lisa?"

Jack shook his head sadly. "As I said, I'm not like you guys. The only weird thing I have is this birthmark on my shoulder." He pulled the neckline of his sweater down and leaned forward, revealing the mark to the brothers. "And I have a pretty good memory."

Kace's eyes widened. "That looks just like—" He pulled the leaf from Bruno's box and compared it to the mark on Jack's shoulder.

"Aunt Greta would know if there's something here," Kace said. "When we find her, it'll be one more question to ask."

Jack leaned in close to the boys, keeping his voice low from the girls. "Did you find your aunt when you went out? I know you didn't go out just for food."

"We found the right place, but we don't know if she's still there. The grouchy lady who opened the door sent us away," Orion said. "Tomorrow we'll try again."

Jack noticed how Orion's eyes lit up when he spoke of his uncle. "You always speak so highly of him," he said. "Sounds like he's a fascinating man."

Orion let out a yawn and stretched. "If you don't mind, we can talk about Bruno more another time. I'm exhausted, and I'm sure you guys are too. It's getting late, and tomorrow will be a long day. We'll have to figure out how to survive here without money or food."

Kace, getting the attention of the girls, said, "We'll need to keep our powers hidden for now, even here in the house. All that light might attract unwanted attention. Besides, it's late and you two need to be in bed." He then sent them into one of the bedrooms and waited for the door to close.

As for him and the other boys, they made a place for themselves to sleep there in the main room, laying out some extra blankets. They weren't taking any chances of being caught by surprise were the king's soldiers to figure things out. Each comfortably in his spot of choice, Orion said goodnight and blew out the candle.

While within minutes Orion and Kace were snoring, Jack, unable to sleep, lay back staring into the darkness.

Then just as he thought it best to close his eyes, he thought he saw a thread—not of light, but something decidedly magic—there against the darkness. It ran along the ceiling, down the middle of the room and over to the wall, and then down to the fireplace, where it seemed to disappear between two of the stones below the mantle. He got up and padded quietly to the fireplace, not wanting to wake the others.

Once there, he traced the magical thread to the stones where it led. Pushing on one stone and then the other, he discovered the top one was loose. He then found by moving it side to side he was able to coax it little by little from its place. Finally when he had moved it enough, he used the tips of his fingers to pull it all the way out. There behind it was an open space and deep within it was a bundle. He removed it.

The prize in hand, he quietly made his way in the dark back to where Kace and Orion were sleeping. Striding a bit too far, he accidently stepped right on Orion. Disturbed, Orion blurted out, "What the—?"

But before he could say any more, Jack shushed him not wanting to wake the girls, and said, "I think I found something! I need light."

It took Orion a moment to fetch the small box of wooden matches from his pocket, get one lighted, and then find the candle. With the flare of the light and the stirring about, Kace, too, awoke. "What's all the fuss?" he asked.

Jack held up the package for both to see. It was wrapped up neatly with cloth and twine.

"What is it?" Orion asked.

"I don't know," said Jack. Hooking his thumb back toward the fireplace, he added, "I found it behind a stone. There was this magical thread of light or something leading to it. I saw it when I was laying back and staring at the ceiling."

"Wow," said Kace. "That's one of Bruno's tricks. But how'd you see it? I mean, even Orion and I would miss it unless he told us it was there—which he didn't, by the way."

Jack only shrugged. At that moment, he didn't know and really didn't care. He just wanted to see what was inside the wrapping. "Let's open it," he said.

"Give it here," said Orion. But then softened his tone when he saw Jack's reaction. "It might have a magic protection, is all. Safer that one of us opens it up."

Jack gave Orion the small bundle and Orion quickly undid the twine. Unfolding the cloth, a wide smile broke over his face. "It's a wad of money. I can't believe it. Uncle Bruno comes through again. Now we have no worries. We can buy whatever we need. No more going hungry and sharing sandwiches. Won't the girls be surprised when they wake up tomorrow morning and find a big breakfast?"

Kace smiled and patted Jack's shoulder firmly. "You may not have powers, but there's something special about you— I can tell."

Jack smiled, relieved that he was able to help out finally. "But what does this mean?" He asked. "Why was I the one to see that light and find the money?"

The twins looked at each other and then back at him. "That, my friend, is exactly what we need to find out."

LOOKING FOR SUPPORT

Once the woman at the Fairyton Institute left the twins at the door, she made her way back to one of the school's parlors. Moving slowly down a dusty narrow corridor, the elderly woman passed by the library noting that the principal, Gretuala, was still awake and looking through a dusty pile of photo albums.

Gretuala looked up at the old woman and smiled. "Is everything all right, Sindia?"

"It's nothing, madam. Just some strange boys asking for someone named Greta," said Sindia, snorting at the annoyance. "These outsiders are just trying to get inside the building. It's been the same for all the years I've worked here. They'll use any trick, won't they?"

"Did they seem sick?" The principal felt her heart speed up at the familiar name.

Sindia shook her head. "I don't think so, but they looked identical to me."

Principal Gretuala turned suddenly pale. "Goodnight, Sindia. I feel very tired."

Only her family called her Greta, and it had been years since she heard that name. She rushed outside to see if she could catch them before they left, but nobody was there. Dejected, Gretuala went back inside. It was too risky for her to wander around outside at night, so it would have to wait until morning.

She didn't sleep well that night, tossing and turning and trying to picture the boys as they would look all these years later. Come morning—the bright green leaves on her bedside plant predicting a sunny day—she began looking for clues in her past. In a pile of papers, she found the old picture that Bruno drew of Greta and her sister the day they went to the city fair for the first time. A gifted artist, Bruno had them stop in the middle of the road so he could draw the sketch. She scanned the drawing, her eyes fixing on the tiny and weathered cottage off in the background. Something about the structure tugged at her, and with no other clues, Ms. Gretuala decided to go into the city and see if it was still there.

With no one watching, Greta slipped out of the school. She took a carriage and directed the driver to let her out a few blocks from where she remembered the cottage to be. Once on the street, she took care not to be followed. When she reached the spot she was looking for, sure enough the old cottage was still there.

As she made her way to the front door, out jostled Kace and Orion off to the market. Orion, more intent on his brother than where he was going, ran right into her, almost knocking her over.

"Oh, I'm so sorry. Are you all right, madam?" Orion caught Greta by the arm, holding her steady. She found herself staring directly into his sparkling blue eyes; they were the same as her sister's.

Kace, following right on Orion's heals, recognized the woman in Orion's grasp instantly and gasped.

"Aunt Greta, is it really you?! We've been searching for you!"

Gretuala's breath stopped for a second. She knew these boys. "My darlings!" she gushed, throwing her slender frame at them both, wrapping them in her arms and kissing them lovingly. "I hoped more than anything that it was you at my door yesterday." But then catching herself, she dropped her voice to a level just above a whisper. "Please, one of you must meet me at the café on the corner in fifteen minutes. All three of us can't be seen together. It's too risky"

Kace nodded to Orion. "I'll go. You already had too much excitement yesterday with those soldiers."

Even though Orion wanted to meet with Greta as badly as his brother, he didn't want to argue and agreed. They both looked back where Greta had been standing, but she was gone.

A few minutes later, Kace found himself sitting at a table near Greta at the café across the street, while Orion was off at the market buying food for everyone.

Greta was sitting at the corner table pretending to keep her bright-blue eyes focused on the newspaper in her hands and sipping an orange juice that the waitress just brought over. Kace, sitting across from her and at a different table, casually stared at the menu while scanning the room. It was a cozy café with a colorful and cheerful interior. The menu was full of traditional food.

Greta kept a calm exterior, but inside she was quite excited. While Kace was looking at the menu, she used the family's form of silent communication and asked him to speak without being noticed.

"I'm so thrilled to finally see you with my own eyes. You've got your mother's good looks. Are you boys all right? Do you have everything you need?"

"We're all right for now, but oh, Aunt Greta, we've been looking for you. Everything has changed so quickly. Uncle Bruno disappeared, but we found our sister, Aunt Greta. We found Lisa and a boy who says he's her brother. We're all together again." The words were pouring out of him almost as quickly as he could think them.

"You found your sister? But how—"

"We're not safe, Aunt Greta. The Sheevali soldiers are after us. They found our house in the woods, and they saw our shield powers. I'm not sure we'll ever be safe again."

At that moment Greta's eyes grew watery and hot tears began running down her face. She dropped the newspaper involuntarily, wiping the wetness from her cheeks.

"Is everything all right, madam?" The plump waitress stood over Greta looking concerned. Greta looked up and smiled sweetly. "Yes, of course. I just remembered that I have to leave, though. Let me pay you for my order." Greta made a point of rummaging through her purse slowly, searching the bottom for imaginary change.

"I don't feel comfortable at this café. I feel like people are starting to become suspicious of us, and the waitress keeps eyeing us. We have to regroup and figure out our next plan of action. In the meantime, we need to protect your sisters. The other boy with you, send him to the school with your sisters at six tonight. He will have to tell the guards that

Principal Gretuala is expecting him. I'll enroll them under my protection. They will have to hide their powers and the fact that they are sisters. They can't know who I am, but they'll be safe." Greta found her change and dropped it into the waitress' hand and smiled. "Keep the change. For your trouble, dear."

"Jack will bring them. I'll make sure of it," Kace said with determination.

"Stay hidden in the house until tonight. I'll come again at midnight to answer your questions." And with that, Greta was gone.

WHITE LIES

By the time Kace came home, Orion was pacing back and forth outside of the cottage with two big sacks of potatoes, a couple loaves of bread, and huge jar of milk propped against the front door. On the ground nearby was a stack of firewood and a sack with used clothing for Jack and Lisa. Orion gave him an expectant look.

"How did it go? What did she say? Will she help us?" The questions kept popping out of him.

"She's taking the girls into her school to protect them. We need Jack's help though. The woman who answered the door last night might recognize us if we take them."

Orion poked his head into the house. "Jack? Can you help me carry these things inside?"

Jack came out, leaving the girls to play on their own. Ever since they'd learned of their powers they'd been connected at the hip and lost much of their care for the rest of the world. They didn't even notice Jack leaving.

Jack came outside and, seeing Kace, gave Orion a quizzical look.

"Sorry, brother, we needed you alone." Orion gestured toward Kace who looked at Jack pleadingly. "We found our aunt."

Jack simply nodded. "Okay, now what?"

Kace cracked the door open and checked on the girls. Lisa and Alexa were sitting in a conspiratorial way, whispering secrets into each other's ears and giggling. Kace closed the door quietly and turned back to Orion and Jack. "We'll explain it later when we're alone, but we need you to take Alexa and Lisa to Aunt Greta's school tonight. She's going to take them in, but the staff can't see us with them. If we go, it'll be like handing ourselves over."

Orion piped in. "What about Greta? We need to talk to her."

Kace gave them an I-know-something-you-don't look. "She's coming here at midnight. Greta's going to help us, but we can't tell the girls who she is or they might be compromised. I've come up with a story. But you guys have to play along."

Jack and Orion exchanged looks. "What can we do?" Jack asked.

Inside the house, Kace sat Lisa and Alexa down. "We've found a safe place for you to hide. You're going into the Fairyton Institute. It is the most prestigious school in the kingdom and a great opportunity for you both."

Alexa's face screwed into an unconvinced frown. "How did you get us in? We barely have enough money to eat. Did you find our aunt?"

Kace shook his head. "Unfortunately not. Yesterday, when Orion and I went out, we saw a man attack a woman and try to take her purse, so we saved her. She turned out to be the principal of the Fairyton Institute. She's the one who told us that Greta doesn't work there anymore. She wanted to thank us in some way, so we said that we have two little girls with us and we have no money. Today when we bumped into her again, she told us that she thought about our situation and promised to take you in."

Deep frown lines appeared across both girls' faces, and Lisa pursed her lips. "That seems like a very fortunate meeting." Alexa looked Kace full in the face and raised a questioning eyebrow.

With a nervous laugh, Kace pushed on. "It'll be safe there. You'll have to hide your powers and your relationship, but at least you won't be on the streets." He gave Alexa a hard look. "Now don't go looking a gift horse in the mouth. Beside, you know what the Sheevali king will do to us if he finds us."

The girls looked at each other and shrugged. They knew their brothers had their best interests at heart.

Jack cut in and addressed Lisa directly. "The soldiers are already looking for Kace and Orion. If they learn you're also twins, they'll hunt you as well. For now, you'll have to keep your powers secret. Promise me?"

Lisa pulled Jack aside. "I know you're looking out for me. Whatever you do always comes out of that good heart of yours. I love you, Jack."

He looked at Lisa and gave her a sweet smile. "Hey, I have something to show you. Close your eyes, OK?" Jack picked up his backpack and started rummaging through it.

Lisa leaned toward him, peeking inside the dark cavern of his backpack. "What is it?"

Jack snapped the bag shut and gave Lisa a look of mock indignation. "I said close your eyes, peanut, or I'm not showing you anything."

Lisa folded her arms in front of her and huffed, but she closed her eyes and waited. Jack went back to rummaging in his bag and pulled out something he had wrapped in a soft sweater. He unwrapped it, revealing the camera he'd hidden away. He gently pulled her hands out straight and put the camera in them. "You can open your eyes."

Lisa opened her eyes and gasped. "Are you serious?! You love this thing."

Jack looked at her sheepishly. "It's an early birthday present."

Lisa squealed and gave Jack a huge hug. "This is the surprise that you were talking about at home, right?"

Jack hugged Lisa tightly. "Yeah. I want you to have it. I'm sure it'll come in handy. And when we get back home, we can look through your photos and watch the videos together."

Watching Lisa's delighted face, Jack felt a cold chill run through him. He wasn't sure now if she belonged with him in the real world or if one day he was going to have to go home alone. The magical connection with Alexa was so apparent, he couldn't help but wonder if in time, she would slip slowly away from him forever.

EVIL FRIENDSHIP

Grinage stabbed angrily at a steamed carrot on his plate, while across from him, a military man—broad across the shoulders and long in limb—watched the king with sharp grey eyes. He was clean-shaven, with sharp boney cheeks, and thin lips with a calculating and sly smile. As not to betray his amusement at Grinage's means for dealing with anger, he turned his head ever so slightly and casually rearranged the long sandy ponytail, spotted with grey, which fell between his shoulder blades. At least, he thought to himself, he's not turning members of his staff into garden decorations.

"Blast it all!" Grinage growled, the orange vegetable sliding off onto the table. "How could those dimwits have lost a pair of children?!"

Sebastian fought back the urge to smirk and instead adopted a look of deep concern. "That is troubling, Your Majesty."

Grinage grunted and continued his vegetable massacre by moving on to a slice of zucchini. "I think we found the royal twins. I saw them myself, but I didn't recognize them at first. I trusted that fool, Captain Orlando, to bring them to the castle instead of orbing them here myself, and that idiot let them escape. They're adults and quite capable of finding their sisters, if they are to be found. I can't take the chance of all four of them reuniting as foretold. We have to find them, and I want them alive."

Sebastian, too, had reason for annoyance at the news. Those twins were a threat to his own plans as well. His son Antuan was set to marry Grinage's daughter, Bella. With her eighteenth birthday fast approaching, the public announcement was only a matter of time. Together, they would make a powerful alliance, and through their children would flow the blood of two different universes. –Not to mention that his place in the king's court would be that much stronger.

Grinage's voice imposed upon Sebastian's musing. "Any ideas on how we can capture the twins?"

Sebastian considered for a moment. "I think it's time to pay close attention to the Fairyton Institute in the city. With my sister Greta running the school, it would be a likely place for the twins to seek help—even if they haven't yet found their sisters. I think that we should plant another spy."

A smile crept over Grinage's face. A low laugh rolling out of his throat, he leaned forward and pointing a thick finger at Sebastian, said, "Every time I speak to you, you prove yourself useful. You are the only one that I can truly trust." He then rose from the table. Walking to the window, he motioned Sebastian to follow.

Sebastian stood and stepped confidently toward the king. There together looking to the mountains in the distance, he couldn't help but recall the day he had stolen the medallion from the Zilonia kingdom and surrendered it to King Theodore, Grinage's father.

He was alone in the middle of a grassy field just outside of the city, covered in the blood of his beloved, when the Sheevali soldiers found him. He was hustled aboard a stark and monochromatic spaceship and within seconds was hurtling from the planet's surface and into space toward the Sheevali home world.

It seemed only minutes when the hatch to the ship again opened and he was staring out into a colorless world. With his beloved Jasmine forever taken from him, Sebastian immediately felt a connection to the flat, cold-looking Sheevali kingdom.

Escorted from the ship, Sebastian was led inside a large white room with high black pillars. One of the black-clad soldiers accompanying him directed his gaze toward a door at the far end of the hall.

Just then, two soldiers walked in escorting a tall man with two younger men following close behind. All three men wore long white coats. The older looked to be in his sixties, but his long, blonde hair and piercing, black eyes made him no less imposing than a young man in his prime. The other two men were close to Sebastian's age and didn't look at all alike.

A herald announced the men, calling out, "The King of Sheevali, Theodore, and his two sons, Prince Grinage and Prince Christopher!"

Sebastian bowed his head in respect and presented the jar with the long-awaited medallion inside to the king. Theodore chuckled. "Jasmine told me a lot about you, Sebastian. It's a shame that she is not here to share our joy at this great victory. She was a valuable servant." Theodore motioned to the guards standing behind him and the two men stepped forward. "As I promised, you and your son can stay here with us. My men will walk you to your new chamber where your son is waiting for you." At that, Theodore turned on his heel and strode out of the long room with his sons, leaving Sebastian in the uncomfortable presence of two glaring guards. A bad feeling settled into the pit of his stomach.

As soon as Sebastian was settled in his new place, he was summoned to join Grinage for a hunting trip. Although the prince made Sebastian uneasy, the trip was still a great opportunity to see the mysterious coasts of his new home.

During their journey, Grinage remained silently sullen, which only heightened Sebastian's discomfort. Sebastian, wishing to establish a bond with Grinage, said, "Your world is so different from mine. There is much less color—actually, there's no color at all."

Grinage let out an annoyed grunt and made a show of ignoring Sebastian completely.

Sebastian chose not to be put off. Instead he pressed on, taking in his new surroundings. "I can't believe how warm it is here. The white makes everything look so cold, but I can feel the heat reflecting from every surface. Everything looks so glossy, like it's made of glass."

Grinage spun around and glared at Sebastian, "We're just trying to be classy here."

Sebastian's eyes lit up with laughter. "Was that a joke? I knew you weren't just a stuffy prince." Sebastian grinned at Grinage. "You Sheevali are very different than Zilonians. If it is not inappropriate, I'd like to learn more about your powers?"

Sebastian struck right at Grinage's pride, and the prince's hubris would let him do no less than brag about his special abilities. Grinage looked at Sebastian with a sneer. "My power is better than whatever your silly Zilonian blood lets you do. I can send any object hurtling like a cannon ball wherever I choose. I could knock down a house with a field of pumpkins. You're no match for me."

Just then, a large scale-winged beast burst out from over the trees and dove at them. Its nostrils flared with fire and the smell of brimstone poured from its mouth. As it dove, it pointed its razor-sharp horns and the stacks of arrows protruding from its head down at Grinage and Sebastian. It was joined by a second.

Sebastian's eyes went wide. "What are those things?!"

A low chuckle escaped Grinage's throat. Turning on Sebastian, he growled, "Those are your dates for lunch. You better hope they make it quick!" Cupping his hands to his mouth, he shouted, "Welcome, Arrowzavers! Come and get it!"

Grinage and his soldiers pulled camouflage hoods over their heads, making themselves invisible and started to run back to the castle.

Sebastian stood in shock, realizing suddenly that the Sheevali king's betrayal meant his death. Sebastian cursed himself for ignoring his instincts. Thinking fast, he stripped his cape from his shoulders, exposing the bright red lining underneath. But the richness of the color in such a colorless world wasn't enough to distract the Arrowzavers from attacking. Instead, the beasts lowered their heads and let loose their arrows.

Sebastian activated his powers just in time. He transformed his red cape into a shield as hard and impenetrable as steel. The weapons speeding down upon him were deflected harmlessly away. One by one they landed scattered around him, protruding up from the ground at haphazard angles.

Undeterred, the two Arrowzavers let out an ear-splitting shriek and an army of the creatures responded, filling the sky overhead. As one the nightmarish flock sent wave after wave of arrows down thick and heavy upon him. But just as before, they could not reach him.

However, more than a few bounced from the field about him, glancing this way and that. One pierced a guard through the chest. He fell dead. Another went full into the prince's shoulder. Grinage fell to the ground in pain. Sebastian saw him go down, and, almost as if he couldn't help himself, he ran to the prince's side to keep him safe.

Soon the Arrowzavers ran out of arrows. Sebastian, seeing all the barbs lying about, leaned into Grinage's ear and whispered, "It's your turn, brother."

With a nod of agreement and a wave of his arm, Grinage sent the arrows straight back at the army of Arrowzavers hovering and shrieking above them. One after the other their bodies fell from the sky and landed with sickening thuds.

Grinage looked around at the scene before him and clasped Sebastian's hand in his own. "I owe you my life. My father didn't trust you, and he wanted me to leave you here to die. These creatures have been terrorizing our kingdom for centuries. But thanks to you, they're all gone. I will speak to my father on your behalf and ask him to make you my general."

Sebastian, chuckling to himself at the memory, looked to Grinage who was staring back with a nostalgic expression of his own. Suddenly a crash and the sound of Bella and Antuan arguing in the hallway came booming through the walls.

Grinage let out a laugh and patted Sebastian on the back. "Just like us when we first met, eh? It will be no time before their relationship blossoms just like our friendship has. Soon Bella will be eighteen, and our children can finally be wed."

He then gave Sebastian a conspiratorial wink. "Now let's talk about that spy we're going to send to the Fairyton Institute."

Sebastian smiled, realizing just how far he had risen in Grinage's esteem since those early days. Now totally trusted, he could afford to take risks and create a plan that was so cunning and cleverly crafted that nothing would be able to stop it.

FIRST DAY AT SCHOOL

Just before sunset, Jack, Alexa, and Lisa found themselves standing in front of the ivy-covered gates to a huge mansion. Nervously, Jack knocked at the door and waited. A moment later, the face of a guard appeared out from a small window. "Yes? What's your business?" he barked.

"I'm Jack, and these girls are my friends. We're here to see the principal, Ms. Gretuala. She's...uh...she's expecting us." Jack hardly believed the words himself as he said them.

The guard consulted a sheet of paper and nodded. "Looks like you check out. I'll take you to her." The guard walked them through the gate and across a green lawn to the front entrance. The main door opened to a waiting room from which an inner door, protected by more guards, led into the main part of the school. The guard led them through the halls and up a flight of stairs until they reached Ms. Gretuala's office.

Ms. Gretuala was waiting for them with her assistant. Her face was calm and poised, devoid of anything but professional detachment.

Jack stood next to Lisa and Alexa, hovering over them protectively. He looked at the principal of the Fairyton Institute with a level gaze, but he couldn't help but shift nervously on his feet. "It's nice to meet you, ma'am. My name is Jack, and this is Lisa and Alexa. They've been living on the streets with me and the other boys. I'm very grateful that you're giving Lisa and Alexa the opportunity to stay here."

Ms. Gretuala responded firmly, "Thank you, young man. I'll make sure to take care of them. You may say your good-byes and then leave."

Jack stayed only long enough to say a cheerful good-bye and then spun on his heels and left. The door closed at his back before had taken a second step.

Lisa and Alexa stared at Ms. Gretuala's tall frame. Her full lips and bright, round, blue eyes betrayed nothing of her thoughts or emotions. She had a naturally slender shape, and her long chestnut hair piled atop her head in a high up-do only made her look taller.

Greta scanned them for a moment, saying nothing. The girls began to fidget under her heavy gaze, only gaining relief when she pressed her lips together in a rigid line that was neither a frown nor smile. "In order for you girls to stay here, you must follow our rules. You will also have to share a room, though I trust after living on the streets that won't be a problem. My assistant, Ms. Clarantia, will give you a tour of the school grounds." Greta motioned toward the petite woman standing behind them. Ms. Clarantia was a curvy woman with a wide waist. Her brown hair was pulled back into a tight bun that pulled at the corners of her mouth, making her smile appear strained and uncomfortable.

Ms. Clarantia bit her lip and cleared her throat with a polite cough before she spoke. "Follow me, girls. I'll show you to your room."

Alexa and Lisa scurried after her as she led them down a long, wide hall with many doors. Most of the doors led to rooms that housed two girls, but a few were for only one student. After what seemed like an endless row of door after door, Ms. Clarantia stopped and let them into a small room with two identical beds, wardrobes, and desks. Fresh bedding and uniforms lay on the beds waiting for them.

"Go ahead and get changed. I'll be back in a few minutes to show you to dinner." Saying no more, she walked from the room and closed the door behind her.

Moments later, Lisa and Alexa had changed into their new uniforms—identical full-length black dresses edged in a fine, white lace that matched the white undershirt. The bodice was fitted with fasteners and a long belt that shone like silver.

The girls set to work investigating their new room while they waited for Ms. Clarantia. It was a brightly decorated space, with large windows looking out over the well-maintained yard. A knock heralded the assistant's return, but when Alexa and Lisa opened the door, a meek-looking little girl was standing beside her. The girl's hair was tied into a pretty side braid, giving her a sweetly feminine look, but her deep-chocolate eyes were rimmed red with recent tears.

Ms. Clarantia shoved the girl forward. "Girls, this is Nia. She's one of the students here. I had to stop by her room to get her because she refused to go to supper with everyone else." Nia seemed to tremble at Ms. Clarantia's words, and she kept her gaze planted firmly on her feet, never looking up to meet the girls' eyes.

All of the girls fell in line behind Ms. Clarantia as she led them to the dining hall. Alexa noticed that Nia was dragging her feet and that a thin sheen of perspiration was forming on her forehead. Nia began to fidget nervously as they came closer to the room. Alexa tried to ease Nia's tension by striking up a friendly conversation. "Nia, right? Why didn't you want to come and eat with everyone else?" But the girl said nothing while big tears began streaming down her face.

Lisa was watching Alexa's unproductive efforts and saw that it only made the matter worse. Now the poor girl was trembling and couldn't say a word at all. Lisa pulled her sister away and whispered in her ear. "Just leave her alone. She'll come around when she's ready."

When the girls walked into the dining room, Ms. Clarantia showed them their seats by the corner of the last table. Most of the students were almost done with their meals and many were leaving. Lisa and Alexa looked around, seeing a grandly spacious room lit by the fading sunlight that streamed in through large, high windows. From their seats, the students had a mesmerizing view of the mountains just outside of the city.

While Lisa and Alexa sat captivated by the view, two girls walked up to Nia. One leaned in and whispered something into her ear. With a squeak, Nia dropped her silverware and ran from the room crying. The girl who'd spoken watched Nia go with a satisfied smirk, and the two girls turned to each other and fell into a fit of giggles.

Alexa screwed her face into an indignant frown, not liking what she'd witnessed. She turned on the girls and glared at them and then made her voice as commanding as she could. "What did you say to Nia?"

The tall girl with frizzy hair who'd done the speaking turned and sneered at Alexa. "It's none of your business, and if you put your little nose where it doesn't belong, you'll find yourself in the same position as Nia."

Lisa moved to stand between Alexa and the girl, but as she moved forward, she tripped over her shoelace, spilling her drink all over the chubby, hostile-looking girl beside her. The girl looked down at her uniform in disbelief and then turned a disapproving expression toward Lisa. Rolling her eyes, she looked toward her tall companion. "Beatrice, don't even bother with these losers. We'll make sure they get what they deserve later."

Ms. Clarantia saw the girls arguing and rushed over to put herself between them. She looked at the smaller, rounder girl and frowned. "Fiona, why are you wet?"

Fiona adopted a wide-eyed innocence as she spoke to Ms. Clarantia. "We only wanted to introduce ourselves to the new girls and offer them our help if they needed anything. They just attacked us out of the blue. Did anyone evaluate them before letting them in? I'd hate it if their next attack hurt someone. We didn't do anything to them and they just became violent."

"Thank you, Fiona. Girls, you need to follow me."

Alexa cried out with indignation, "They are lying! I—"

Ms. Clarantia interrupted Alexa with a wave of her hand. "I don't want to hear anything you two have to say.

Follow me." Ms. Clarantia turned and stormed out of the room with Lisa and Alexa trailing behind her. As the doors to the dining hall closed, they could hear Beatrice and Fiona giggling behind their backs.

Ms. Clarantia led them back to Ms. Gretuala's office up on the second floor. Unlike their previous visit when the room presented as elegant and inviting, this time it was shaded by the girls' worries.

When Ms. Clarantia opened the door, Ms. Gretuala was at her desk working on a stack of paperwork. Ms. Clarantia pushed the girls in and announced loudly, "These two are out of control. They've already become violent, and it hasn't even been a full day since they arrived. There's no room for these girls in our school. They just attacked our two best students when they were offered help." She looked at Lisa and Alexa and continued. "We've punished students for a lot less in the past. I don't want you to think that you can get away with such behavior."

Ms. Gretuala's face looked grim. "Thank you for informing me, Ms. Clarantia. You can leave the girls with me. I'll deal with them. The assistant principal left the room, glaring at the girls on her way out. Ms. Gretuala got up from her chair and stared at the two sisters.

Lisa and Alexa knew that they'd messed up badly. Alexa steeled herself and gave Ms. Gretuala a pleading look. "We're so sorry that we gave you a bad impression. We just didn't like the way Fiona and Beatrice treated Nia. She ran out of the dining hall crying without even eating anything after Beatrice whispered something in her ear. She was so scared. We just wanted to know what Beatrice told her to make her that upset."

Lisa started to cry. "I didn't mean for my juice to spill onto Fiona. I stumbled over my shoelace and it splashed all over her dress."

Ms. Gretuala kept her face stern, but there was no anger in her eyes. She walked closer to them and leaned against the front of her desk. "I know you're telling the truth, but bad manners and misbehavior will not be tolerated at our school. I'll take care of this incident for you today, but you must be very mindful from now on. I may not be able to help you next time."

Lisa wiped away her tears. "Thank you for believing us. We won't let you down."

Ms. Gretuala rang the bell that summoned the assistant principal. Ms. Clarantia came to her office immediately. "The girls shouldn't be causing any more trouble, but just in case I'm giving them a warning. I want to give them a chance. They've had very little food and sleep in the last two days, and with the new environment that's enough to make anyone act up. I'll be keeping an eye on them personally." She looked at Lisa and Alexa pointedly.

"Yes, ma'am," Ms. Clarantia scowled.

Greta smiled at the girls once Ms. Clarantia had left. "You can go to your room now. Stay out of trouble on your way." The girls darted out of the office and out into the hall.

When Lisa and Alexa had retreated back to their room, Alexa pulled Lisa close into a furtive whisper. "Ms. Gretuala was very kind to us. She believed us right away. It was kind of strange, don't you think?"

Lisa nodded. "You're right. I don't think our brothers would bring us here if they didn't trust her. She must be connected to us somehow."

Alexa grinned. "Do you think maybe they found her?"

"Who?"

"Our Aunt Greta! Now it makes sense that she didn't ask Jack a lot of questions. She probably has a reason for not saying anything to us."

Lisa's eyes sparkled at the intrigue. "I wonder..." is all she said.

MEETING AT MIDNIGHT

The clock was ticking seconds away from midnight, and the boys could hardly contain themselves. They paced around the tiny house, trying to quell their excitement. They had so many questions about their parents and family, and the answers were only moments away.

The subtle crunch of gravel outside the front door signaled Greta's arrival. Orion and Kace lunged at the door all at once to let her in. They rushed into her arms, letting her envelop them in a hug she'd wanted to give them for years. Tears welled in her eyes and she let out a great sigh. Finally she could release her emotions. Greta looked at Kace and Orion again and hugged them with all the strength she had in her body.

Even though her nephews had already transformed into young men, the habits she remembered in them as children were still there. Orion had that same serious face and furrowed brow that she'd always teased him about. She'd warned him it would lead to worry lines, and sure enough he had grooves along his forehead to prove it. Kace took after his father, Christopher. She saw it in the easy way that he brushed his hair back with his left hand. She smiled at the memory of him as a boy mimicking his father's every move.

"I'd always dreamed of the day when we'd see each other again. And now I can't believe that it's here." Greta exclaimed. Kace and Orion beamed at their aunt and thrilled in her embrace.

Greta looked up from her nephews as if noticing the third boy, the one with the black hair and familiar eyes, for the first time. She gave him a wary smile. "It is very nice to meet you again, Jack."

Greta was still concerned that there was a stranger among them. She didn't know anything about him aside from that he was Lisa's brother, and that gave her little reason to trust him. Sebastian had taught her that shared blood doesn't always mean loyalty. She waved him over to her with a grim look. "Come here and let me look at you." Jack hurried over, hoping to make a good impression. He knew that he would need Greta's help if he and Lisa were to ever get home.

Greta looked at Jack's lean frame, then reaching up near as high as she could, she put her right hand above his head. She caused a warmth to spread through her body and then let it pass into Jack.

Starting at the crown of his head and pulsating down to the tips of his toes, Jack felt as if his body had suddenly grown lighter than it had ever been, and when he looked down he saw that he and Greta were floating just above the surface of the floor.

Greta then began circling Jack, her feet never once touching the ground and her speed growing until she became a blur of motion. All of a sudden, a shudder went through her body and into Jack's, passing the powerful magic between them.

Her task done, Greta came to a halt in midair. The magic ebbed away slowly, dropping them gently back to the worn floorboards.

She stood silently for a minute before a grim smile spread across her face, then turning to Kace and Orion, who were watching their aunt anxiously, she said, "He's fine." She put her hand gently on Jack's shoulder. "Since you're my niece's brother, you're a part of our family. We will protect you as well."

Jack blinked and stared at her, looking confused. "What? I'm not even sure what happened, but you're OK with me?"

Greta nodded. "If you weren't one of us, you'd have gotten quite a shock from that magic and dark vibes would be coming from you. We're all from the Zilonia kingdom's royal family, which means we all have powers. You already know about our ability to communicate silently. I can tell when people belong to either the Zilonia kingdom or the Sheevali. I can also tell if someone is telling the truth or if they're lying. I could have even sent you into a deep sleep."

"So, can you make one of those power shields too? I saw Kace and Orion doing something like that when I first met Alexa."

"No. That's a power that only the twins have. But, everyone in our family is immune to the shield. We can pass through it as if it's not there."

Greta's face became grim. "I feel strong vibes coming from you, Jack, but I can't tell what they are. I feel you have a very close connection to our family, but I need more time to figure it out. What I know now is that you don't belong to either of the universes. You need to be very careful. We can block our minds using our powers if the Sheevali king tries to read them. You, on the other hand, are an open book to him. He could read your mind very easily. I can feel that there's a reason you're here with us, and we can certainly use all the help we can get. You might not even realize it, but you're already a valuable asset. We need information, and Kace and Orion can't go outside without raising suspicions. There must be some way to get you into a position where you can gather information for us."

"I'll do anything I can to help, but I don't know much about this world," Jack replied with uncertainty.

Greta thought for a moment before coming to a decision. "I'll help you get a job at my friend's tavern. You'll be able to hear everything that is going on in the city and keep us informed if the Sheevali officers spill something important. If you come in contact with the Sheevali king, Grinage, you'll have to drink a memory-erasing potion. I'll brew it for you. You understand that we have to be sure that our secret stays safe."

"Erase my memory? Isn't that dangerous? How can I go on if I forget about Lisa?"

Greta gave a comforting smile. "Please don't worry. The potion only works for a short time—a few hours at the most— depending on the dosage you take. You'll hardly notice your memories are gone. You'll be fine."

Jack hesitated, his brow furrowed. "I'm not sure..."

Greta smiled, "Don't worry, Jack. We will look out for you; I can sense that you really need to do something very important. You are a protector, I think, but more than that, you now have the opportunity to be a spy."

Jack's face lit up. "When do I start?"

THE KING'S AGENDA

Grinage looked out the window and as always was fascinated by the gorgeous garden below. The space was alive with sparkling fountains in every color of the rainbow. A lush, grassy lawn was divided into islands of rocky garden peaks, each punctuated by crystal fountains, some in bizarre human form and others stranger still. It was his pride. Anyone who disobeyed him or made him mad, he would turn into a fountain. The fountains were worth much more to him in this form than the beings were alive.

At one time he punished those who displeased him by means much more dreadful. He would turn them into slugs and bugs. But doing so made his beautiful daughter angry. Each time she learned of a new victim, she would stare him down, her warm brown eyes, almond-shaped and long lashed, turned agate hard and cold. She'd then surrender the graceful ease of her dancer's frame and stomp off, her backbone rigid and stiff.

When he finally brought up the subject, she'd turned on him in a huff.

"I can't stand the way you treat people when you're angry with them!" She yelled, a petulant pout showing on her pooched lips. "How can you expect to gain the people's respect when you turn everyone into insects? How am I supposed to know if an ant is just a bug or if it's my poor handmaid? You even turned my piano teacher into a slug without telling me why. It's infuriating, Father!"

It was true, Grinage had turned Bella's maid into a bug as punishment for shattering a delicate vase, and the piano instructor simply annoyed Grinage with his constant playing. Grinage never liked art the way Bella did. He only tolerated it for her sake. But far from feeling remorse at her chastisement, the king simply delighted in the shock of black hair framing Bella's flushed face.

He opened his arms out in supplication. "Please don't start with that music teacher again! He was an incompetent fool. And you know that maid of yours was nothing more than a hopeless klutz. I can't let these types of behaviors go unpunished. So what can I do? Do you have another way to punish my subjects when they misbehave?"

At this Bella smiled brightly. "You can build a beautiful garden filled with fountains. Anyone deserving punishment can work back into your good grace."

He'd agreed immediately if only to appease her. It wasn't long afterward that the witch appeared in his court with a spell for creating precious stones from the souls of the people he would change into fountains.

He remembered how the witch from the Valley of Soovers came uncomfortably close to him and, before he could react, she yanked a single piece of his hair, murmured something under her breath, and made the hair disappear in flames. She then told him that he had the power to turn people into fountains. She explained that if he collected thirteen different gemstones, including a pure, pear-shaped diamond, he could create a loyal servant in the shape of a great beast.

This beast would protect him from any harm and give him the ability to conquer both the land and the sea. If Grinage would simply climb onto the back of the beast, he would be able to swim under the ocean without needing a single breathe and he would be able to understand the language of the sea creatures. There was one condition, however—all of the gems had to spring from the souls of human beings; they had to be the reflection of the true heart within each victim.

Grinage thought it was nothing but the ravings of a mad woman. In exchange for this new ability, the witch had asked that he grant her marriage with the man of her choice. Grinage would not be commanded by anyone, so he threw her out of his castle and forgot all about the disheveled crone.

Then he transformed his first handmaiden. She became a shining crystal fountain at the heart of which was a precious stone. He knew then and there that Bella's suggestion had been fated. Each time afterwards he'd experience a surge of power and excitement more intense than the time before. As his powers grew, so did the beauty of his perverse creations, the shape of the fountain owing to the victim's own spirit, the water flowing from it the color of their soul and emotion, and the gem stone the measure of their hopes and dreams.

When Bella found out about what her father was doing, she was horrified that he'd twisted her beautiful idea into something mean and hideous. Grinage knew that she feared the strength of his magic and wondered why she cared about these servants. They were nothing to him, little more than bugs, but he had shaped them into something incredible; surely she should have been happy? They were his servants to command after all, not hers.

Smiling to himself at the memory, the king's gaze wandered beyond the valley and out into the mountains. He ruled the entire city and all the land, but he couldn't put his hands on the mountains or the Tiger Cave where his younger brother Christopher and his sister-in-law Juliana had taken refuge.

Grinage was gnawing silently on his daydream when a knock disturbed him from his pleasure. Turning around, he saw Sebastian waiting patiently in the doorway.

Sebastian gave Grinage a quick bow. "I found a spy as you asked. He is called Poison Rufus, and he lives up to the name. He is an expert in brewing poisons. The Fairyton Institute is looking for a gardener, and Rufus is the perfect person for the assignment: he knows every herb and flower by heart. He can assassinate anyone you desire using but the nail on his pinky finger. All he has to do is put a few drops of his nail poison onto whomever you wish, and his spells will direct the brew's power."

"He sounds promising," said the king calmly, approving the general's choice. "You are loyal as ever, Sebastian. I hope this candidate is better than the other ones you brought to my attention before."

"He has another useful power, if you'd like to see it. He is here now. Would you like to see him?"

Grinage waived his hand, summoning Rufus in.

Sebastian opened the door and Rufus glided inside. He was wearing a long hooded cloak that shrouded his body and most of his face from view. He had a long pointy nose and heavy-lidded eyes. He made a circle and stopped in an obedient position in front of the king, a friendless sneer playing on his lips. As he came to a halt, dusty spider webs made of thin metal wire and intricately woven appeared out of nowhere and covered all of the candle stands.

The king looked around at Rufus's handiwork and smiled. "Very impressive. Now get rid of the nets," he reprimanded his servant with an affirmative tone.

Rufus whispered an incantation under his breath and blew on the webs. They all disappeared at once.

Grinage turned back to his work, but continued to address Rufus in a firm voice. "You will answer directly to me. If you can't reach me, and you have something urgent, the general is your next contact. He will come and find me if your news is worthy enough." Grinage waved his hand absentmindedly. "Now leave."

The man bowed again and quickly left.

After Rufus was gone, the king looked up from his work and addressed Sebastian. "I think he will do well for us— better than the one we have inside now in any case. I have a very strong feeling about this lead. I want you to place more spies among the magic school's staff. The more eyes and ears we have there, the better."

Sebastian made a mock bow behind Grinage's back. "As you wish."

"This time," Grinage growled, staring back out of the window, "I will find them. I can feel it in the very core of me, and when I do...oh, yes, when I do, they're all going to pay!"

THE LEGEND

Despite the lateness of the hour, everyone was fully awake. Soft moonlight shone through the thin curtains on the windows while a cheerful fire crackled in the hearth. The three boys sat around the table with Greta and pretended to sip at steaming mugs of tea. Greta drank deeply, letting the liquid warm and soothe her throat before she spoke. "I know you have a lot to ask. Listen closely, and I'll answer any questions you have left after I'm done." She took a deep breath and began her tale.

"For centuries, our ancestors ruled the Zilonia Kingdom and we lived in harmony, love, and prosperity. Our castle was the centerpiece for the Zilonian people. Unlike the hideous decorations the Sheevalis have given it, the Zilonian castle was bright with light colors and was a trademark of the city despite being heavily guarded."

"But in the time of your grandparents' rule, the sky grew very dark and thousands of black ships came upon our world. It was the Sheevali King Theodore with his two sons, Grinage and Christopher—your father."

Kace's fist came down hard on the table, his face a mask of anger. "Our father is one of them? We're related to that beast Grinage?"

"Kace, please!" Orion hissed. "Let her finish. Don't forget that it makes us Sheevali too, along with Lisa and Alexa. That alone should prove they're not all bad."

Kace crossed his arms, but remained silent as Greta continued.

"The Sheevali King Theodore arrived in our land and made it his mission to conquer it. The Zilonian army was strong, but Theodore owned the only thing that could overpower us: a magic medallion that he wore on his neck.

"The medallion that Theodore wore was special. It could clone any powers for the person wearing it. It was made of crystal-clear diamonds set in the shape of a coiled serpent. Two deep-green emeralds act as its eyes, and a bright ruby sets off its slender tongue. It's overflowing with powerful magic, making it visible from far away. It shines so brightly that it can't be hidden, and it is even visible beneath clothes and armor.

"But great power always comes at a price, and the medallion is incredibly dangerous. When it is used, it radiates an intense heat that will burn and blister the skin of whoever uses it. Depending on how it's used, it can only be worn for a short time. The magical jewels must be cooled off in a special jar that rejuvenates the medallion's power and calms the churning energy once used.

"But the medallion is not the only item with great power. The jar, though made of very plain and simple brass and carrying marks from years of use, creates a strong healing elixir. The jar heals anyone who would use the water within and infuses the medallion with great healing power.

"It is said that every one hundred years the medallion will grant immortality to the person who possesses it and permanently will transfer the powers that were collected within. At that time, the energy emanating from the medallion will be so strong that it can open any door—including the door to the cave in Tiger Mountain behind which your parents are currently living."

Kace jumped up in his excitement, knocking his chair over. "Wait a minute, you're saying that our parents are alive? Bruno said they disappeared without a trace."

Orion quickly added with desperation in his eyes, "Does this mean we can save them?"

Greta gave Kace a stern look and waited to continue speaking until he was sat firmly in his chair again. She sighed and replied, "I know Bruno wasn't clear about this matter, but at that time, you were too young to understand the complexity of what was going on and, frankly, there was nothing you could do. But now, the ordained day is soon approaching. The Sheevali Kingdom is waiting for it because the Sheevali king wants nothing more than to rule the entirety of this world unopposed forever. Without a Zilonian heir fighting his every move, he'll have exactly what he wants.

"There was a time when this medallion belonged to our family, but one day it disappeared from our secret chamber. It was stolen by King Edward's older son—my brother Sebastian. One day they both just vanished. We couldn't have known that Sebastian intended to betray us, but the brutal death of his sweet beloved convinced us of the depth of his depravity. We knew nothing more of him until

Theodore arrived at the edge of our land wearing the medallion and intent on conquering our world."

Kace burst out anxiously, "Please tell us about our parents."

Greta smiled at Kace's impatience and continued, "When the black ships came upon us, your father was one of the finest Sheevali officers. Christopher had a very valuable power. He could redirect other people's powers away from him, making him essentially immune to any magical attacks. He and his brother, Grinage, tricked your mother, Juliana, and captured her. Before sending Juliana to the Sheevali prison, Grinage used the medallion to copy her orbing power, sucking away her energy with it. Your father saw the princess fading away and it broke his heart to see how fragile she was. Instead of delivering Juliana to his father, Christopher was swept away by your mother's rare beauty; his very nature changed in her presence and he fell in love with her."

Greta stared at the boys, her eyes sparkling with unshed tears.

"He told his brother that he would take Juliana to the castle but instead, he brought her back home to her family. If not for his love, he would have delivered her up to King Theodore; but it seems they were fated to meet. I, of course, had to check Christopher's intentions first and I soon learned the purity of his plans for my sister. It wasn't long after that your parents married.

"But while your parents found happiness, the Zilonia kingdom was being divided by the Sheevali army. Amidst the terror of their bloody conquest, you boys, Kace and

Orion, were born. It was a glimmer of hope for the people of Zilonia.

"When your mother was expecting for a second time, we learned that again it would be twins. Two sets of twins were exceptionally rare for any family, but your sisters' birth also carried a special omen. The truth is, your parents belong to two different magical universes. There is an ancient legend that says if two pairs of twins are born from parents hailing from different universes, an absolute power will manifest on the twelfth birthday of the youngest siblings."

Greta reached out to hold Kace and Orion's hands.

"You must be aware that this ability is more powerful even than the medallion that King Grinage wears around his neck. With it, you children could throw off the shackles of the Sheevali conquest and unseat that wretched king. You and your sisters have the ability to create the absolute power."

Kace's chair tipped over again and he fell on the floor. Rubbing his head he interjected, "Alexa and Lisa's birthday is around the corner. We need to tell them about it."

Greta raised her hand to calm him down, "I will, when the time is right. The most important thing right now is to keep all of you safe. You have never been more at risk than you are at this time. You can see that?"

Kace nodded, shivering.

Jack's eyes went wide. "I thought what you did earlier was powerful enough," he said. "Now you're telling me there's something even stronger?"

Greta nodded gravely. "It's stronger than anything anyone in Zilonia has ever known. Those who hold absolute power can grant any power to anyone, or take any power from anyone. But most importantly, should it ever be needed, it has the power to generate an energy field strong enough to shield the entire kingdom. The Zilonian people long for the security the rumored twins could create.

"When your sisters were born, only the closest members of our family were allowed in the castle. Outside of your parents and King Edward and Queen Marina, your uncle Bruno and I were the only others present. We limited the serving staff and told only a tight circle of people, but the news somehow made its way to the Sheevali king." She said regretfully.

"The King of Darkness knew then that the Zilonia kingdom had a way to take the medallion away from him and once again become the most powerful kingdom. It was a matter of time.

"He decided to act quickly and attack us with all of the force he had before your sisters turned of age. He would kidnap you all and eventually take your powers for himself. When he attacked our kingdom, the protective shield was broken by the medallion's power. King Edward was killed. It was obvious that Zilonia didn't have a chance against the Sheevali king. Your parents decided that the best thing for you children was to separate you and hide from the Sheevali king. Your grandma could change people's faces. She put a spell on Bruno to make him look old and completely unrecognizable. Alexa and Kace went with Uncle Bruno, and Lisa and Orion were supposed to go with Silvana, your mother's maid.

"Just as the two carriages were about to leave, Orion noticed Lisa crying. She'd forgotten her favorite bear, so he ran back to get it for her. It was too late though. The Sheevali soldiers were already in the castle. Your mother caught Orion and put him in the first carriage with Kace and Alexa. Your carriage escaped without incident, but Lisa's was later discovered abandoned and destroyed. In our grief and fear we decided to go into hiding separately and cut off all communication. We thought it would be the best way to survive the Sheevali king's wrath.

"After King Edward was killed, Queen Marina passed the ruling status on to your parents. Juliana and Christopher became the new king and queen. Queen Marina told your mother about the secrets Tiger Mountain held and how it could keep them safe. But entering the cave in Tiger Mountain meant not returning for a long time. The way is sealed until the medallion reaches its one-hundred-year peak or the fated twins create the absolute power. After they entered, the mountain sealed itself and within it everyone's magical powers. There beneath the mountain, time no longer affects them—they are the same as the day they entered the cave."

"Why didn't our parents take us with them?" Orion asked, a tinge of hurt in his voice.

"If you came with them, you wouldn't be able to develop your powers and the Zilonian legacy would be lost forever without any chance for survival."

Jack wrinkled his brow and tried to analyze the situation out loud, "If King Grinage is in charge now, then where is his father Theodore?"

"After conquering our beloved kingdom and destroying everything we loved, Theodore left his son Grinage in charge of the Zilonian lands under mysterious circumstances. I'm not even certain if they still communicate. Grinage became the new Sheevali king and took complete control of Zilonia. But his cruelty has proven even greater than Theodore's, because Grinage—even after all this years—is desperate for his father's love and acceptance. He always believed that Theodore could not love him as much as he did the son of his own flesh, your father. Grinage feels that sting potently. It drives him ever onward in his quest for power.

"He's tried many times since to gain access to the cave in Tiger Mountain, but he doesn't have enough power to open it. Instead he has set guards at the mouth of the cave to ensure that you and your sisters never reach your parents. Most of all, he is afraid that one day the four siblings will find each other and, reaching a certain age, they will bring his kingdom down."

When Greta finished her story, tears were streaming down her face. But she looked lovingly and hopefully at the boys as if a huge weight had been lifted from her. Kace and Orion drew closer to her in comfort, hugging her and brushing the tears from her cheeks. When her tears finally ceased, Orion broached a sensitive question.

"Why didn't you join our parents in Tiger Mountain? Aren't you afraid that King Grinage will find you?"

"It was decided that it wasn't wise for all of our family members to be in one place. We were afraid that if King Grinage were ever to get inside of Tiger Mountain, he could destroy the entire family all at once. But the king knows that I live and work here. He no longer feels threatened by my life. I signed away my right to the Zilonian throne. In return, he promised to let our school exist without his control. You may think me a coward, but I needed to protect my girls too."

"Aunt Greta, do you know how to activate the absolute power? How are we supposed to know what to do when the time comes?" Orion said, a worried look spread across his face.

Greta shook her head sadly. "Until now, the absolute power has only been a legend. It is something sacred, but mythical...for the moment anyway. It is a mystery that you and your sisters will have to resolve. If it really exists, all of our futures depend upon it. "

"No pressure then," Jack commented wryly, suddenly realizing the enormity of the task ahead of them.

Greta smiled. "Sadly, there's every pressure. I wish I could change this treacherous journey ahead. I wish I could smooth the pathway forward or guarantee your success. But..." her eyes glistened with tears. "Failure is likely to end in death...for all of us."

Kace was quiet, contemplative, then, "We know our history now and what it cost you and everyone in our family." His voice was calm and sincere. Yet his determination was clear. "We may only have a very slim chance to change the destiny of our kingdom, but we'll do everything possible to save our family."

He stood up, pounding his fist down hard on the table. "We need a plan." Greta smiled at his enthusiasm, a spark of hope in her eyes. "I agree, but we can't make one tonight. If I don't return to the school soon, someone will start looking for me. I'm sorry that I didn't have time to answer your questions tonight, but I will see you tomorrow at the same time. We can continue then."

She made her way to the door, looking back with pride at her family. "I have more hope now. Maybe things will be different very soon," she promised. "We will be able to overthrow Grinage, and our family will be united once more!"

NIA

Lisa and Alexa were trying to get comfortable in their new school. On their first morning there, the school had its usual assembly. All of the students gathered together in neat rows on the grand lawn outside the main building where the sun shone bright in a clear blue sky. The girls marveled at the beautiful flat lawns and elaborate gardens in the magic school and tried to take in their new surroundings amid the excited morning chatter.

When Ms. Gretuala walked on stage, a practiced hush fell across the congregation of girls. She smiled brightly at all of her students and began her morning announcements.

"Good morning, students. It's good to see you on this lovely day. I only have a few announcements for this morning. First, we have two new students joining us today. Lisa, Alexa, will you stand beside me on stage?"

Lisa and Alexa looked at each other a moment and gulped simultaneously. Together they walked to the stage and stood beside Ms. Gretuala. All of the curious faces staring up at them made them feel rigid and uncomfortable, but they smiled sweetly and tried to appear confident in front of the gathered crowd. They could see Fiona and Beatrice glaring at them from the front row.

Ms. Gretuala continued. "Please be sure to welcome these girls and make them feel comfortable here. I want every student who studies at the Fairyton Institute to have a pleasant learning experience." She turned and smiled at them, spreading her arms wide. "Welcome, girls. Please treat this school as your home. Now, you may return to your places."

Fiona and Beatrice continued to glare at Alexa and Lisa from the first row. After the events of the evening before, they couldn't believe that Lisa and Alexa hadn't been punished.

Beatrice leaned over and whispered into Fiona's ear. "These girls are going to be a problem. I have a feeling that we're going to have some real trouble with them."

Fiona squeezed her little fists and nodded in response. "We'll have to show them who's in charge here."

Lisa and Alexa left the stage and stood next to Nia, giving her big grins. Nia flushed red and put her head down, grabbing both girls' hands in appreciation of their friendship. The girls stood together and listened to the rest of Ms. Gretuala's morning announcements.

When everyone was dismissed, Nia guided them to their first class, filling them in as they walked. "Where are you girls from?" Before Lisa and Alexa could come up with the answer, Nia kept rambling on. "Most people here come from money. The school is very exclusive. I only got in because my father has been friends with Ms. Gretuala for many years. This school doesn't take in many tavern owners' daughters."

Alexa and Lisa shot each other furtive looks before Lisa piped in with Kace's story. "We were living on the street with some other kids. Ms. Gretuala agreed to help us after our friends saved her from being robbed. We didn't have anywhere else to go."

Alexa leaned close to Nia, intentionally changing the subject. "We were worried after you ran off. What happened yesterday? Who are those two girls?"

Nia sighed, and a look of shame crossed her face. "The tall one is named Beatrice, and the other girl is Fiona. Beatrice and Fiona are cousins, and Ms. Clarantia is Fiona's mother. They always pick on me because they think that I don't have any magic powers." Suddenly Nia dropped her voice to a conspiratorial whisper. Together they ducked into an alcove away from the other students. When she was sure that no one else was listening, she continued. "Yesterday when I was passing their room, I overheard Fiona and Beatrice talking about a plan to steal Ms. Gretuala's magic pen. They want to use it to add more points to their names on the board and win the best-students competition."

Lisa looked at Nia quizzically. "It's just a game. What's the point of that?"

"It's because the prize is fantastic. Students work as pairs, and only one pair can win. Whichever team wins will get to go into the room where Ms. Gretuala keeps magic animals. No one is allowed to go into this room except our teachers and the winners of this competition." Nia sighed. "I heard it's amazing. Can you imagine all the wonderful creatures that might be in there?"

Speaking about the animals had brought Nia's voice to an excited squeak. She checked herself and went back to a low whisper. "Gabriella and Chantelle are getting very close to winning. They're the only real competition for Fiona and Beatrice, but those two don't want to leave anything to chance. They're going to use their powers to trick Ms. Gretuala. Their plan is to take the pen from the principal's office today during lunch. When I was passing by, they saw me. They said that if I tell anybody about their plan they'll make my life miserable. They will find a way to expel me from school—"

Alexa cut in, determination bubbling up in her words. "What powers do Beatrice and Fiona have?"

"Beatrice can reach through walls and open any door, and Fiona can make water run. Their plan is to fake a huge plumbing problem to distract Ms. Gretuala and get her away from her office. While Fiona uses her water power, Beatrice will steal the pen and make the changes on the board." Nia became quiet for a moment as if in thought, suddenly she blurted out. "I do have magic powers, you know. Everyone here does. It's just that mine is a little strange. I don't like to show it to other people..."

Lisa brightened up. "What is it? I'd like to see."

The corner of Nia's mouth turned up into a nervous grimace. "I can make people's speech impossible to understand. They begin to stutter."

Alexa clapped her hands together and laughed. "That's so great! You can make Fiona and Beatrice look like fools in front of the entire school!"

Nia's face flushed, and she shook her head so vigorously, Alexa and Lisa thought she'd hurt herself. "We're not allowed to use our powers in school without proper supervision, but I suppose it would be funny."

"I have an idea!" Lisa blurted out. "Let's teach these girls a lesson. I have a little camera, and I can record Fiona and Beatrice cheating on their scores. That way we'll have evidence that they're up to no good."

"Um, what's a camera?" Alexa asked with a perplexed look on her face. "It sounds weird."

"It's like a magic instrument, but it can be used by anyone." Lisa grinned. "It can record anything it's pointed at and then play the event back again."

"Can we see it?" Nia asked, intrigued.

Lisa nodded and the girls ran together to Lisa and Alexa's room. Lisa pulled the camera out of her backpack and held it up for the girls to see. "Jack gave it to me so I could video animals and take pictures of my trip. It was supposed to be a surprise."

"That little thing can record whatever I see? It's so strange!" said Alexa curiously examining the device.

"How does it work?" Nia exclaimed.

Lisa giggled. "You point this part, it's called the lens, at whatever you want to record. The camera captures the image and sends it here." Lisa pulled the memory card from the camera so the girls could see it. Then you can play it back any time you want. It's like replaying a memory in your head except other people can see it too."

Alexa gave Lisa a conspiratorial grin. "You'll have amazing memories from this trip."

Nia didn't know what the girls were talking about, but then Lisa started showing them how to work the camera. She held it up to her face and adjusted the wide lens.

"You just twist it like this until you get the shot you want and press this button. The camera records everything just like that."

"That's easier than I thought. No wonder anyone can use it!" Alexa said, her eyes shining.

Nia couldn't contain her excitement. "My room is just across the hall. We can regroup there after we catch them in the act."

Alexa nodded in agreement. "Lisa, you should follow Beatrice since you know how to work the camera. Nia and I will keep an eye on Fiona to make sure she doesn't spot you spying on Beatrice." They all agreed just as the bell signaling the beginning of classes rang throughout the school.

"I don't know if we should..."

"Shhh, Nia. It'll be fun," Alexa laughed. "What could go wrong?"

THE ARGUMENT

Every Friday, King Grinage and his beautiful daughter Bella enjoyed a special tea time together. The King treasured that time because Bella, on those occasions, would create a new set of tea china for them to use. She loved art and beauty, and showed off her special talents and patience when decorating the cups and teapot.

A few years ago, Victoria, one of her mother's servants, gave her a set of magic coloring pencils. Victoria cherished Bella and knew that the young lady liked to draw patterns and color them on her walls. So on one of Bella's birthdays, the kind servant approached the princess and handed her the box. They'd colored together that day, and Victoria showed Bella how to use the pencils' special powers. Ever since then, Bella hadn't been able to put them down.

No matter what mood she was in or what kind of day she'd had, all Bella had to do was pick a plain china set and make it beautiful with her new tools. And if the results didn't suit her, a simple shake would send the colors spinning away into a new pattern. Bella treasured Victoria's gift and the world it opened for her with all her heart.

The princess busied herself in her room, expecting her father to come in and present her with new china at any moment. She moved about her quarters, tidying up the little messes her art had made on the various tables. Bella was drawn to natural hues, and her quarters reflected that with their earthy palette and sophisticated furniture. As she bustled about from the bedroom to the sitting room, and then through the entry, she delighted in catching little glimpses outside her large windows of the beautiful valley below the castle.

Her father arrived with a knock on the door. She swung it open with excitement only to stop short, scowling. This time her father wasn't alone. Antuan stood beside him and gave her a cocky grin.

"Good afternoon, princess," he said arrogantly and let his tall, muscular frame sweep into a flourishing bow. At six feet tall, Antuan's toned form towered over Bella's lean frame. But as he bowed close to her, she could see the flirtation in his sparkling eyes. As he smiled, his grey eyes grew even smaller and his thin brown pony tail fell over his shoulder like a rat's tail. He walked past her into the sitting room with his long nose held high and a confident swagger in his walk.

Bella watched Antuan and spun on her father, fury in her eyes. "I thought this was our time! What's he doing here?" She clenched her fists, and her dark-brown eyes grew nearly black.

The king smiled and hugged his daughter in an effort to calm her anger. "You're right, Bella. Normally it is. But today, I want you to spend time with your future husband. I hope to announce your engagement soon, and not long after that you will be married. Like our tea time you will need to come up with your own traditions with Antuan. I'm confident that you can accomplish this."

"But, Father!"

"Not another word, Bella! I am your father, and you will do this because I asked you to." The king's tone grew tense.

Bella slammed her open palm down on a nearby table. "You can't possibly—"

"That's enough, Isabella! My decision is final." The king's face was hard with rage. After a moment his features softened and he then kissed his daughter on the forehead before leaving.

Bella watched her father leave, an angry scowl playing on her lips, before turning back to Antuan. She eyed him warily while he paced about the room. They had known each other for many years, but never really got along. He had a reputation among the palace women that Bella found scandalous. She knew that someday they would likely be married but before today, she hadn't taken that very seriously. She'd always thought that she would be able to change her father's mind.

Antuan curled his lip and strutted over to the table where he picked up a piece of her china. "The person who gave you this junk shouldn't be working in the castle. There's no room for tacky stuff in a place like this." He tossed the cup back onto the table contemptuously, letting it clatter loudly.

Antuan thought he could impress Bella with his taste, but she only glared at him with rising fury. Bella's cheeks grew red and she clenched her teeth as she spoke. "You ignorant, cocky fool. You have no brain. There is no way that I will ever marry you! Go back to chasing the servant girls, and don't ever come near me again!"

Bella threw her hands over her face and muttered a silent spell. When she opened her hands, her beautiful face was that of a screaming monkey. She hoped that Antuan would be disgusted and leave, but instead, he laughed.

"You can change your face any way you want, but I know that you're beautiful! It doesn't matter if you don't like me. Our parents have already arranged our marriage. You'll be my wife whether you like it or not!"

Antuan slammed the door behind him, and Bella could hear his laughter as he walked down the hall.

TRACKED

Now that the boys knew their destiny, they tried to gather as much information as they could about their heritage. First, however, they had to find the exact location of Tiger Mountain. Finding the mountain would be dangerous. Greta warned them that the Sheevali Kingdom's guards were watching like hawks.

Kace and Orion sat at the table discussing their ideas while Jack lay on the floor thinking of Bruno and the leaf-shaped crystal. The box in the burned cottage hadn't left his thoughts for days. Just then, Orion snapped his fingers and smiled brightly. "Let's go to the library and see if they have a map. With a better idea of the terrain, we can make a plan on paper and then sneak out at night to the mountains to check them out."

Kace nodded gravely then looked at Jack. "Do you want to come with us or stay here and watch the place? We might need someone who isn't identical."

Jack smiled and sat up. "I'd love to. This city is so big, and I want to see it. Let's go. Who knows, maybe we'll find something there about Bruno's leaf."

Kace grabbed his wallet and tucked it into his back pocket as the boys left the house. They turned and walked toward the café where Kace had met Greta the day before.

As they passed the café, the waitress cleaning the outside tables accidentally bumped into Orion, dropping a stack of napkins all over the ground.

"Pardon me! Let me help you with those." Orion stooped down and helped her pick them up. He handed the stack of napkins to the girl, and she gave him a flushed smile.

"Thank you," she replied with a flustered tone.

"Come on, Orion!" Kace yelled from down the road. "We're going to leave you behind!"

The young girl, Elsa, looked up to see Kace waving at the boy in front of her. Recognition sparked in her mind. She remembered him from the day before. He was the strange boy who sat in the café and didn't bother ordering anything. She looked back at the boy who had handed her the napkins and realized that he was identical. They were twins.

After Orion ran off to join the other two boys, Elsa went inside the café and told the owner about the twins she just saw. "Mr. Bruce, do you see those boys over there?" she said, pointing. "One of them was here yesterday acting suspicious. Do you think they might be the twins that the Sheevali king is looking for?"

The large man with thin curls at the back of his head watched them. Stroking at a nasty wart on his chin and imagining his purse fat with gold, he said, "Let's follow them and see where they go. I have to be sure that they're the twins the king is looking for. The king will be angry with us if we send his guards chasing the wrong twins. And maybe, if we can learn what they're up to, we can claim a bigger reward."

A woman's cry rose up out of the kitchen, and Bruce's wife called out to him. "Bruce! There's a fire in the kitchen!"

Bruce let out a sigh and darted into the café, calling back out to Elsa, "Just go and don't wait for me. I'll keep an eye on their place."

DISTRACTION

Everything in the city was new to Jack, but strangely he felt that he'd been there before. He took in every single light, house, and street corner with glee, while trying to pinpoint why the city seemed so familiar. Suddenly, it struck him. Jack had seen the city before—in Ms. Solunski's house. The paintings lining the wall were images of the city surrounding the Sheevali castle.

"I've seen this place before. Ms. Solunski had paintings of it hung on her walls."

Orion rolled his eyes at Jack. "This neighbor of yours looks more suspicious by the minute. Don't you agree, Kace?"

Kace just sneered, "I wouldn't trust her, that's for sure."

The smell of fresh-baked bread and pastries drew Jack in as they passed a bakery, and he pressed up close to the glass to catch a better look at the shop's display. When he looked into the bakery window, however, he noticed in the window's reflection that a young lady with a round face and a small, pointy nose was staring at them. He leaned toward Kace beside him and kept his voice low.

"Don't look now but it seems we have an audience. It's the girl from the café."

Kace and Orion bristled at the revelation. "We need to lose her," Orion whispered through clenched teeth.

"It'll be strange if we don't go inside now. We've been staring at this bread for too long." Kace smirked at Jack, but there was concern in his eyes.

The bakery was in the heart of the city. It resembled a cozy little cottage, and the alluring smell of fresh-baked bread wafted out onto the street. Inside, the fragrance was intoxicating as the scent of wonderful muffins, warmed refreshment, and scrumptious cookies and pastries mingled together into a heavenly aroma. Kace and Orion sat at a table next to the window with a clear view of Elsa's conspicuous form.

"We're all right in here for a moment," Orion said, trying to act as if nothing was wrong. "But we need to split up. We're too conspicuous."

Jack remained standing with an eye on the layout of the bakery, searching for a way out. He leaned in close and kept his voice low. "I think I can slip out the back and find the library on my own if you can keep her busy."

Kace and Orion looked at Jack together. Kace nodded gravely. "We'll take care of it, brother. You just get what we need." Jack winked at the twins cheekily and snuck out the back of the shop.

Elsa was outside the front of the bakery, waiting for the boys to leave. Kace took a close look at her and smiled. "I've got this," he told Orion. He got up and went outside, walking right up to her.

"You can come and join us, you know. You don't have to watch us from the street."

The girl flushed red, and Kace was encouraged to give her his most cavalier smile. "What's your name? Such a lovely girl probably has an equally nice name."

"Elsa" she said quietly "I, uh...um..."

"Mine's Kace. I recognize you from the café."

The girl—trying to hide her embarrassment—said, "I remember you too. You looked very flustered."

"We're new in town, and I got lost yesterday. I didn't know what to do, so I just came into your café. It seemed like a nice place, but I didn't have any money. I'm sorry that I took up your space."

"That's all right!" Elsa's voice came out as a frightened squeak. "It's common for people to just spend time in the café."

Kace offered his arm out for Elsa to take and she slipped her hands around the crook of his elbow. "Can I make it up to you? Come on and take my invitation."

Kace walked Elsa inside the bakery and joined Orion at the table. "This is Elsa. She's very shy, so be nice to her." Kace winked at Elsa and watched her reaction.

"Hello again. It's a pleasure to meet such a beautiful girl. I hope I didn't cause you too much trouble when I dropped those napkins on the ground. Can I use this as an apology?" Orion smiled and offered Elsa a muffin with a glass of milk that he had ordered from the counter.

Elsa stumbled over her words, her face growing the color of a ripe tomato. She lowered her gaze and said contritely to Kace, "I-I thought that your behavior was a little strange yesterday. Today, when I saw you with your twin brother, I assumed that you might be the twins that the Sheevali king is looking for. My boss—the guy at the café—he sent me after you to check because the king's soldiers have been going door to door telling everyone to report anything suspicious. They said that the twins they're looking for are local, know the area very well, and have special powers."

Kace let out a nervous laugh. "If we're the twins that the Sheevali king's looking for, would we really be outside in broad daylight looking at all the sights?"

Orion kicked his brother's foot under the table and then in silent communication, said, "It was dumb to go outside during the day."

Kace frowned, knowing that Orion was right.

Orion tried to flash his most charmingly boyish smile at Elsa. "I hope we won't get held up by soldiers, because that would definitely ruin our trip. You have such a fascinating city. I'd love to get the chance to see all of it."

The flush to Elsa's face grew worse. She couldn't believe how mortified she felt about following these charming boys. It was clear they weren't a threat, and their good looks sent her a-flutter. "I'm so sorry. I'll tell my boss that you boys aren't locals. You can't be the twins the king is looking for if you're not from around here. Hopefully he'll just forget about you."

MEAN GIRLS

Class was over finally and the students began spill eagerly into the lunchroom. Lisa, Alexa, and Nia placed themselves away from the others with a careful vantage point. They ate quickly, keeping a careful eye on Beatrice and Fiona, determined to catch them in the act. As they watched, they noted the speed at which Beatrice was eating; she wanted lunch to be over quickly. They could almost feel the tension rising up from her in waves. After polishing off the final crumb, she stood, sending Fiona a calculated nod and left the room with Fiona only a few steps behind.

Before the girls could follow, only moments later, a tall, rather skinny student came running toward Ms. Gretuala with a worried look on her face. "The bathrooms are flooding! There's water everywhere!"

At the news, both Ms. Clarantia and Ms. Gretuala ran toward the bathrooms. Lisa, Alexa, and Nia slipped out of the hall quietly, just in time to see Fiona pretend to just arrive on the scene. She followed her mother, Ms. Clarantia, as Ms. Gretuala paused in front of the door to the bathrooms.

Ms. Gretuala looked relieved to see her. "Fiona dear, I need you to stay here and guard this entrance. Don't let anyone else in until Mr. Goodson has fixed the problem. I don't want this to get any worse than it already is."

Fiona smiled at her, obviously quite content to be in charge. "Don't worry, Ms. Gretuala. I will guard it with my life."

As Alexa and Nia passed by they smiled at her, but their feigned warmth didn't reach Fiona as she sneered at them.

"Don't look at me. I don't want you here. I have more important things to do. Go to your rooms and let the important people take care of things!"

Alexa rolled her eyes at Nia in an exaggerated movement and then giggled much to Fiona's disgust.

In the meantime, Lisa had sneakily followed Beatrice to Ms. Gretuala's office. With her camera primed and ready, she had managed to record Beatrice carefully sliding her hand through the door; it looked odd seeing her human arm dissolve through the solid oak door. Lisa couldn't help but watch with some admiration as Beatrice turned its handle from the inside. Then it was easy for Beatrice to just walk right into Ms. Gretuala's office and steal the magical pen from the top drawer of the large desk placed in the center of the room. It was a magnificent writing implement, long and slender with silver scrollwork at its tip that magically changed color based on the holder's intentions.

Beatrice picked up the pen and waved it gracefully. "It's time to make history!" Beatrice exclaimed pompously and walked proudly out of the office.

As Beatrice emerged, carefully scanning the corridors, Lisa hid until Beatrice had turned away and walked down the hallway. She then followed Beatrice into the classroom farther down the corridor where the students' scores were written on the board and concealed herself behind one of the long, crimson curtains that hung from the top of the tall windows all the way to the floor.

Beatrice pulled at the cord hanging to the side of a smaller, darker curtain that hung over an object in the room. She watched as the curtain automatically drew back and revealed the scoring system. With a flamboyant swish, she pointed the magical pen at the board and, in a flash, had added an extra few points to both hers and Fiona's names. Beatrice giggled with satisfied delight as their names magically manifested at the top of the list.

"And that is how the winners were born." She cried with delight.

Satisfied Beatrice cast a glance at the magical pen and gulped. While casting the spell, the pen had turned a murky grey, revealing her dishonesty.

"If I put the pen back now," she gasped, "it will be so obvious to Ms. Gretuala. Fiona will be livid that I screwed up our plan."

Beatrice panicked; she had to set it right, it would be obvious that someone had used the pen to cheat. She turned the pen over and over, desperate to change the grey color of deception. Beatrice was so preoccupied that she didn't notice Lisa hiding behind the curtains with her camera recording everything.

Seeing Beatrice's back turned to her, Lisa suddenly had an idea. She quietly slipped off the small beaded bracelet from her wrist and tore it apart, rolling the beads quietly on the floor before the entrance to the classroom.

"No, you are not getting away with your trick, missy. Not if I can help it." Lisa muttered to herself.

As Beatrice started to walk out, still shaking the magical pen in desperation, she stepped onto the beads and her feet slipped from under her as she scrambled in mid-air before landing straight onto her backside.

As Lisa had hoped, Beatrice had dropped the pen in her fight to stay upright and had left it on the floor as she'd raced out of the room. Guessing that she would realize her error and come back for it, Lisa quickly grabbed the pen off the floor. Concentrating hard on her task, she pointed the pen toward the board, switching the names back to where they had been before. Instantly the magic pen underwent a transformation. It was no longer grey but had resumed its original color.

"That's more like it," Lisa commented quietly.

Hearing Beatrice coming back, she placed the pen quickly on the floor where it had fallen and ducked back behind the curtain.

From behind the curtain, Lisa could see that Beatrice looked hot and agitated. She started searching for the pen, moving tables and chairs and then crept on her hands and knees. Once she'd located it, she sighed with relief that the pen had reverted back to its original color. Beatrice hurried back to Ms. Gretuala's office to put the magic pen back without looking twice at the board.

Alexa and Nia were watching Fiona from around a corner when they saw her cousin rejoin her. At that moment, Ms. Gretuala and Ms. Clarantia emerged from the bathroom with Mr. Goodson in tow. The man was wiping his bald, sweaty forehead with a worn rag. "The pipes are all fixed now. You won't have any more of these nasty little problems."

Fiona and her cousin looked at Ms. Gretuala with eager expressions. "Ms. Gretuala, we kept everyone away from the bathroom just as you asked." Fiona grinned at Ms. Gretuala proudly although Beatrice was still rubbing her backside from her fall. But she smiled angelically at the principal.

Ms. Gretuala gave the girls a tired smile. "Thank you Fiona, Beatrice. It's always nice to get help from you girls."

When Ms. Gretuala had left, Fiona whispered to Beatrice, "Is it done?"

Beatrice nodded victoriously. "There's no way we'll lose now!" she whispered, her voice a low hiss in her throat. Around the corner but watching in glee, Lisa, Alexa, and Nia were laughing quietly to themselves; they couldn't wait for the big announcement or to see the look of shock and anger on Fiona and Beatrice's faces. That would teach them.

THE MAP

Jack walked into the library and looked around at the stunning decor. Adorned like a mansion, the walls were covered in ornate wood paneling, and comfortable reading chairs were scattered about the room in clusters among the overflowing shelves. The main hall featured a graceful, polished marble floor, grand windows, an enormous fireplace, and a sparkling crystal chandelier that hung low from the ceiling in the center of the large, open room. The library was so overwhelming that Jack didn't know where to start.

He looked around the rich space at the shelves and endless books. At this rate it would take him hours to find a map of Tiger Mountain. To his right was a heavy wooden desk. An older lady with her grey hair pulled into a high bun sat behind the desk. He approached and waited a moment while the woman worked on a pile of paperwork stacked on her table.

Jack scanned her nametag and observed the frustrated look on her face before he spoke. He would need all of his charm for this.

He straightened his shirt and smoothed the wrinkles from his trousers before stepping forward. "Excuse me, ma'am, but where can I find the local maps?"

The lady held up her hand, signaling that he needed to wait as she finished reviewing one of the documents. Jack was patient for a few seconds, and then put on his most charming smile. "Glades. What a sweet name," he said exposing his white teeth.

The woman put the papers aside and gave Jack a sweet smile in return. "How can I help you, young man?"

"I'm new in town and I'm unfamiliar with your library. Would you help me find the local maps, please?"

The librarian pointed her finger and a shining gold light appeared, floating toward the shelf where the maps were located. Jack watched the sparkling orb as it floated away and turned back to deliver a grateful grin. "Thank you, Ms. Glades. You've been such a great help."

He passed by the aisle with older books and incredibly ornate, jewel-encrusted volumes. Then he saw two tall shelves, large enough to store thousands of books. One had numerous artifact volumes filled with histories and ancient tales. The other held a large collection of strangely shaped books and some maps, most of them picturing the city.

Jack browsed through them until he came across a very thin, crumpled brochure that showed only mountains and trails. When he opened it up, he was delighted to see that it was exactly what he was looking for. Inside was a map of the Sheevali kingdom and the surrounding countryside. Jack could see the forest where Alexa and the twins had lived in hiding outside of the city. On the opposite end of the map was a high mountain range and the sea beyond. The highest peak was labeled Tiger Mountain, and a river flowed down the mountain in snaking lines until it passed near the edge of the Sheevali castle and fed into the farmlands. He snatched the map up and headed back to the front desk.

Ms. Glades was still buried in her paperwork when Jack stopped by her desk. He smiled and waited politely for the librarian. "Ms. Glades, thank you so much for your help before. I found this brochure on one of the shelves," said Jack, revealing the pamphlet from behind his back. "Do you allow maps to be checked out of the library?"

Ms. Glades motioned for Jack to hand her the brochure, and when he did, she squinted at it closely. The old map looked tattered and worn and unlike anything she would have kept on in the library's collection. "This doesn't look like anything that belongs to the library. It's been too poorly tended. Some other patron must've left it behind a long time ago without any of the workers here to catch it and throw it out. Since no one seems to own it, I think we can call it yours."

Jack's face lit up. "Really? I can have it? I can't believe how kind you're being. Thank you again, Ms. Glades!"

Jack's excitement reflected on Ms. Glade's face, and she let out a girlish giggle. "If only everyone who came in were as well-mannered as you. Is there anything else I can help you with? The library's collection is vast."

Jack grinned and nodded. "I don't mean to bother you, but I was wondering if you know anything about symbolism and where I can find information about the meaning behind certain objects?"

Ms. Glades was enamored by Jack's courteous behavior and smiled openly at him. "What kind of objects? We have many books here, all sorted by subject."

"I'm looking for information on different shapes, I mean. Shapes like flowers or leaves or stones..."

"Hmm, can you please be more specific? Symbolism is a popular subject."

He hesitated, should he explain more? She seemed genuine.

"I've come across some odd shapes, actually symbols really, and I'm puzzled, no, curious. Well, I just would like to know more about them."

Ms. Glades' face darkened. "I'd need to know more young man; I hope it's not dark magic you're planning."

"Dark magic?" He gasped. "No, not at all."

He looked at the huge clock above the fireplace and gave the librarian a worried look. "I appreciate your time, but I really must dash. I'm running late."

Ms. Glades smiled sweetly at him, scrutinizing the sudden change in expression. "No problem, dear. You can come back anytime."

Jack walked away quickly, trying not to run. He didn't want to glance back in case she was watching him with suspicion; he could almost feel her eyes boring into the back of his head. Instead, he took his time tucking the map into his jacket pocket and then casually sauntered away, hoping that he looked relaxed and not like anyone who would be helping the kingdom's most-wanted twins.

THE GARDNER

When Rufus came to the doors of the Fairyton Institute, he met a tall, burly guard at the front gate.

"What's your business here?" The guard glowered at him.

Rufus gave the guard a placating grin. "I heard the school is looking for a new gardener. Can I speak to the person hiring?" Rufus craned his neck over the man to get a glimpse into the school grounds.

The guard straightened his stance, blocking out Rufus's view, and waved at another man. "Liam, go get Ms. Gretuala or Ms. Clarantia. We have someone here who's looking for a job." He turned back to Rufus. "Wait here a moment, and someone will be around shortly."

A few minutes later, a petite young lady came to greet Rufus. She gave him a shy smile. "I'm sorry, but Ms. Gretuala and Ms. Clarantia are both very busy. I'm Ms. Clarantia's assistant, Ms. Sofia. How can I help you?"

Ms. Sofia looked at Rufus uncomfortably. Her youthful face suggested a softer nature. Rufus decided to approach her gently. He gave her an innocent smile. "I'm here to apply for the gardening job. I'm very knowledgeable."

Ms. Sofia gave Rufus an apologetic look. "I'm sorry, but the gardener position was just taken. That's him right there." Ms. Sofia pointed into the school toward a man in green work clothes.

Rufus let the disappointment show on his face. "I suppose I was just too late. Thank you for your time." Rufus turned away as if to leave, but returned to face her. When he turned back, there was a black crow cradled in his hands. "I found this poor bird on my way here. I think it might have broken wings. I have herbs that could heal it, but I need water for them to work. Do you mind taking this little creature with you and giving him some water mixed with this herb powder?"

Ms. Sofia was touched by the old man's kind heart. "Oh, the poor thing! Of course I'll help. Will you come inside with me? I don't want to get the mixture wrong. You can mix it yourself, can't you?"

Rufus agreed, but kept the elation from his face and chose instead to adopt a solemn look. "I'd be happy to mix it. I can wait while you get the water."

Ms. Sofia hurried inside to get water, leaving Rufus sitting on a bench behind the garden, a beautiful indoor conservatory with walls made of thick glass made lovelier by the brightness of the day and the grandness of the protective wall that surrounded the school. The sweetest-smelling roses Rufus had ever come across ringed the edges of the garden and created private alcoves where students and teachers alike could work surrounded in blooming and leafy beauty. As soon as Ms. Sofia turned the corner, Rufus walked over toward the school's new gardener who was planting flowers. Rufus took his gloves off and shook the gardener's hand.

"I'm Rufus. I see you're the lucky man who got the job at this marvelous place. These are the well-tended plants I've seen in years."

The new, yet already stooped gardener was very polite and well mannered. He gladly offered Rufus his hand and introduced himself back. "Isn't this place a beauty? Very nice to meet you. My name's Anthony."

Both men stood silently for a moment and admired the school's luxurious conservatory, its lush emerald landscaping laid out in a welcoming pattern.

Without the gardener noticing, Rufus put a little drop of poison from his nasty nail onto the gardener's hand and murmured something under his breath. At that moment, Ms. Sofia walked in with a glass of water. She looked very frustrated. "I couldn't find you and began to worry."

Rufus apologized, "I'm sorry, I thought maybe there would be water in the garden and when I saw that the door was open, I walked in."

Rufus put the right amount of powder into the water and mixed the medicine together into a thin liquid. When he sprayed it on the bird's wings, the wings immediately fluttered and the bird woke up. Rufus held it gently. "Thank you for your help, dear. I'll just take him outside now." Ms. Sofia showed the old man to the gate with a wary look.

At the gates, Rufus thanked the young lady. "It was kind of you to give me a moment of your time. If you happen to change your mind, I live in the last house down the city's main street."

"Thank you, sir. I'll be certain to tell Ms. Clarantia and Ms. Gretuala to keep you in mind for future openings."

When Ms. Sofia came back, she heard the sound of sneezing coming from the garden. It was the new gardener. His nose was red and his eyes were watery. She ran to him and placed a gentle hand on his back. "What happened? Your eyes are swollen! Let me get the nurse. Ms. Magdalena, please come. We need your help here." Ms. Sofia cried out as loudly as her lungs allowed, not letting Antony out of her sight.

The gardener shook his head in disbelief. "All I did was touch the rose bush. Now I can't stop sneezing. What sort of gardener can't be near his own plants?" Anthony rubbed his red eyes and inflated nose shamefully.

The school nurse, a plump, pale woman, heard the noise and rushed to the garden. She examined the new gardener and clucked in disappointment. "It looks like you're allergic to our roses."

"I have to leave now before my head blows up," said Anthony, holding his forehead.

He bowed his head in sadness. "I can't believe how awful I feel. I've never had allergies before, but—I must admit—I've never seen such marvelous roses before either. I'm sorry, ma'am, but I don't think I'm the right man for the job here. You'll need to find another gardener. Somebody who doesn't have allergies to these beautiful flowers."

Ms. Sofia went back to the gate and found Liam. "Please run and get the man who was just here. We're going to need another gardener after all."

REVENGE

The sun shone bright in a clear blue sky while the institute buzzed with excitement. It was almost time for the big announcement naming the winner of the best-student competition, and all of the girls were gathered in the largest classroom to learn their final scores. As Fiona and Beatrice came down the hall, they heard noise coming from the classroom and saw everyone congratulating Gabriella and Chantelle.

Fiona looked at the board and stopped short when she saw the final score. She sneered at Beatrice, "What did you do? You were supposed to add points to our scores—not to Chantelle's and Gabriella's! I knew I should have done it myself and let you be the guard!"

Beatrice couldn't believe her eyes when she glanced at the scoreboard looming above her. She was positive that she had added the points to their names. "I don't understand what happened! I know I did it right! I saw it change with my own eyes!"

Lisa, Alexa, and Nia were standing behind the door recording Fiona and Beatrice's conversation and giggling at their frantic reactions. Nia waved Fiona and Beatrice over to them while Lisa and Alexa backed away, giving the girls an easy view of the camera's display screen. "I have something to show you. You'll find it interesting."

Fiona was absolutely frantic and began lashing out at Nia. "How dare you speak to me, you powerless loser! You have nothing that could be interesting to either of us!"

Lisa turned the camera so that Fiona and Beatrice could see the video. They were speechless as they watched the strange scene playing out on the camera. In the tiny screen, they saw Beatrice waving the pen and changing the scores on the board. Both girls cowered away from the unfamiliar technology, their faces contorting into a combination of rage and fear. "How did you get this?" Beatrice gasped. "What is that thing? It's lying!"

At that moment, Ms. Gretuala walked through the doors and a hush fell over the group of girls who waited excitedly for the announcement. Fiona and Beatrice distanced themselves from Lisa, Alexa, and Nia and whispered quietly between themselves.

"We have to do something about that horrible device," Fiona hissed. "It doesn't matter who the winner is if we get kicked out of school for cheating on the competition."

"But what can we do?" Beatrice whispered, a sniffle entering her voice. "We don't even know how that thing works. It's so creepy!"

"We have to take it and destroy it," Fiona said.

A cheer went up through the crowd, and everyone clapped for Chantelle and Gabriella. Fiona and Beatrice turned to leave the room, leering at Lisa and her camera as they left. Before they could say anything, Alexa cut them off.

Alexa looked right into Fiona and Beatrice's eyes and hissed, "If you ever go after Nia or us again, we'll make sure that this magic card gets to the principal. Then we'll see who gets expelled!"

For a moment, terror flashed across the two girls' faces, but then their fright turned into seething anger. Fiona and Beatrice gave the girls a vicious scowl, but held their tongues. Fiona stomped her heel and stormed out of the room with Beatrice trying to keep pace.

With Fiona and Beatrice gone, relief spread through the trio for a moment before Alexa turned stern. She took the video card out of the camera. "We need to hide this. I'm sure Fiona and Beatrice will come back looking for it."

"But where can we put it that it won't be found?" Nia whined. "Ms. Clarantia can see through walls. If they get her involved, we're done for, and we need to use this video as leverage against them or no one will believe what we say."

Lisa brightened as she remembered something. "When I was hiding behind the curtain, I saw that a piece of the floor was loose. Let's hide the memory card under it. No one will know about it but us."

"Of course!" Alexa smiled triumphantly. "No one, not even Ms. Clarantia, would think to look for it there." The girls all looked at each other and nodded in agreement. So far so good, but as they hid the card and replaced the cover, they knew that they had to watch their backs, they'd made two spiteful enemies.

A HARD LESSON

Kace was getting nervous while the boys sat in the bakery with Elsa. It had been nearly an hour since Jack had slipped out of the place and gone for the library, and Elsa showed no signs of leaving them alone. Jack could show up at any moment, and they couldn't be caught together with the map. He looked at the big clock on the wall and, using his magic, moved the time an hour ahead. Orion spotted the movement on the big hand of the clock and made the belt on Elsa's waist tighten to make her feel like she'd eaten too much.

When Elsa felt that her belt was getting too tight on her, she rubbed her stomach and pushed the muffin away. "These delicious things are way too much for my figure," she said.

Orion laughed. "I don't think a lovely girl like you has to worry about that sort of thing."

She looked at the clock on the wall and gasped. "Oh, goodness! I've been sitting here with you boys for far too long. Thank you for the muffin, but I have to get going before I lose my job."

"It's no problem," Kace said coyly. "We'll be sure to come by your café again before we leave. I'd like to make up for last time."

"I won't tell anyone about you two, so don't worry about me." Elsa gave Kace a relieved grin and rushed out of the bakery.

Just when Elsa stepped out of the bakery, Jack walked in from the back door with miraculous timing and whistled as he walked to their table. He was holding the map when he took a seat at the table with them.

"Miss me?" He grinned.

"About as much as a cold," Kace retorted and smiled at Jack.

"I see the girl is gone. Have you found out what she wanted?" Jack asked with concern.

Orion let out a tired sigh. "She said that the café owner across the street from the cottage is on to us. She says she's going to get him off our backs, but I doubt he'll listen."

Jack tossed the map to the twins. "It's a good thing I brought this then." Kace and Orion eagerly opened the map and were delighted to see that it was exactly what they were looking for. The trail leading to Tiger Mountain was clearly set out.

Orion looked up from the map at Jack. "Did you have any luck with the leaf? It's got to mean something, right?"

Jack shook his head sadly. "I didn't get the chance. When I asked the librarian about it, she needed more information. I was worried about telling her too much."

Kace agreed. "We all need to be more careful. Leaving the house when we did put us at risk. We should wait until dark from now on unless leaving is absolutely necessary. Even now there might be a better spy than Elsa watching us. We should leave here separately."

"What do you suggest?" Orion asked.

Kace looked at them both. "I'll go first and take the long way back. Orion, you wait about fifteen minutes before following me. Take a different route if you can."

Jack popped a bite of muffin into his mouth. "I have to introduce myself at the tavern and pick up my work schedule. I'll be home later than either of you anyway."

Kace and Orion bobbed their heads in unison. "We'll need to avoid the café from now on," Kace said. "I am sure that the owner will be watching us."

"We must act naturally so that we don't draw attention to ourselves," Orion stated. "It's vital that we watch out for anyone who might be following us. Whatever happens, we dare not lead someone back to the house."

JACK'S MISSION

Jack was excited to work at a tavern. He always thought that it would be fun to have a summer job, but he never expected his first real job to be in a different world. When Jack walked into the tavern, he heard a buzz of conversation. Every table had customers, and the serving staff was running around frantically. Jack took a moment to look around the place. It was a warm and welcoming space. Jack could see steaming bowls of soup and thick sandwiches on most of the tables. The customers all looked happy and comfortable.

A lean boy with a frantic look and a stress-twitch in his right eye walked up to see if Jack needed a table. Jack looked at his nametag and read the name. "Thank you, Billy. But actually I'm here to see Mr. Chapman. I believe he is expecting me"

Billy smiled and took the moment to wipe his sweating hands on the towel at his belt before shaking Jack's hand. "You must be the new guy. Right this way." The serving boy led Jack through the large common room, through the busy kitchen, and past the restroom to a heavy wooden door with an anchor adorning it. "Mr. Chapman is right through there. Just give it a knock." Billy ran off back through the kitchen to continue his work.

Jack knocked, and a low voice floated through the door. "Come in." A tall, strong-looking man with a large nose and penetrating eyes was sitting at the table, reading over some documents.

Jack produced the note that Ms. Gretuala gave him and handed it to Mr. Chapman. "I'm Jack. Ms. Gretuala probably sent word about me. I'm here to help out in your tavern."

The tavern owner put aside the papers and read the note. Greta had already filled him in on Jack's situation, and Mr. Chapman was expecting the boy. He looked at Jack and relief altered his expression. "You have great timing. I'm short on staff today, so you can start now. You can take the two tables next to the window. Billy will help you out."

Mr. Chapman called for Billy, and the same skinny boy who met Jack at the entrance showed up at the door. "Jack is new here. Help him get to know the ropes, and put him on the window tables."

Billy waived his hand for Jack to follow. The young boy gave Jack a pen and piece of paper and pointed at the two tables. "You can start by taking their orders. If someone asks what the most popular meal is, you can tell them that the lamb stew is the chef's special today."

"I think I can manage that," Jack said eagerly.

Jack immediately went to the first table. A short, stocky officer with a hostile expression on his face was sitting there alone. Unlike the other soldiers, who had slung their dark coats on the rack near the entrance or over the backs of their chairs, the man kept his coat buttoned and ready. He was hunched over a black book and wore a scowl on his face. Jack tried to look helpful. "What can I get for you?"

The officer waved Jack away and, with a low, spine-chilling voice, said, "Chef's special."

Jack had a bad feeling about this gentleman. It was like the man was watching everyone there with hatred and distrust. The officer went back to writing in his black book.

Jack moved on to the next table where four soldiers were laughing loudly and swilling a strange, bubbling drink from large mugs. They looked at Jack as he walked up.

"Haven't seen you before. Are you new?" One of the soldiers asked.

"I just started today. What can I get for you?"

The soldiers held up their mugs and sang out their orders in a rising quartet: "Chef's special."

"Chef's special, chef's special, and more cafetoori." They pointed at their mugs.

"We'll take the lamb stew." The soldiers fell into laughter after their song finished. One of the men stood up and stumbled, spilling the contents of his mug on the floor.

The soldier scowled and held out the nearly empty mug. "Drat. I guess I'll need another fill-up of cafetoori too."

Jack had a towel on his belt and he got down to wipe up the mess.

The officer from the next table looked up from his book and snarled at the soldier that spilled the drink on the floor. "You've had enough. There are a lot of troops coming into the city tomorrow, and I need you to be in your best shape to find those lost twins. If you can't speak like an adult tomorrow, I'll have no use for you."

The soldiers looked down at their feet, answering in a chorus of "Yes, sir. Sorry, sir." But the officer continued berating them.

"This drink is preposterous! What kind of drink makes your voice sound like that of a ten-year-old's? It might be full of vitamins, but hearing the way you men giggle over it like children is embarrassing. This drink should be prohibited for all Sheevali men. No one is going to share information with soldiers that sound as ridiculous as you lot."

The soldiers grew quiet and respectfully nodded at the officer's reprimand. When the officer had finished and returned to his book, Jack heard one of the soldiers whisper to the others, "What do you think Officer Seagull is writing in his book? He's always taking notes on suspicious actions or magic, but I don't see anything out of place in this tavern that he could be writing about."

Another soldier leaned into the conversation. "I heard he keeps all of his secrets in there. His memory's not sharp anymore."

Jack finished wiping the floor and ran into the kitchen to bring out the orders. When he came back, Officer Seagull was still there but all four soldiers were gone. The officer looked at Jack to size him up. "So what's your story? I see you're new here. Where do you come from?"

Jack smiled, "I come from a small village down in the valley. I'm apprenticing here to learn how to cook the best food and maybe someday open my own tavern."

The officer smirked. He liked Jack's ambition and decided to make a note of the boy in his book. I need to keep an eye on him, he thought. There's something in this boy's story he isn't saying.

THE INTERVIEW

Ms. Clarantia was busy interviewing for new staff. There had been a lot more burglaries and vandalism in the city lately, and Ms. Gretuala wanted to be certain that the girls in the Fairyton Institute were safe. She had already hired two men for the job, but Ms. Gretuala wanted more.

The broad-shouldered man leaning back in his chair beside Ms. Clarantia sighed as he looked at the list of people left to interview. "We've been at this all day. I haven't been a guard for fifteen years to sit here while you choose all of my employees. I'm itching to get back out there."

Ms. Clarantia gave him a sidelong glance and scowled. "If you think you can do better, Salvador, then go ahead. You can pick the third guard. We'll see who makes the better choice."

Salvador sat up and stretched his large frame, turning his round chin to stretch his powerful neck. "All right. Send in the next candidate."

The Sheevali king sent three of his soldiers to try for the positions. Two were young, very fit men, and one was Salvador's age with a lot of military experience. Unbeknownst to her, Ms. Clarantia had already hired two Sheevali men; only the elder of the three spies was left. His name was Fernando, and his mission was to get in and take over Salvador's position as soon as possible. All three men stood out from the other candidates. They had all the experience and more that the school was looking for. When Fernando entered the office and sat down opposite Ms. Clarantia and Salvador, he figured he wouldn't have to worry about getting the job. Salvador looked at his paperwork and started in on his questions.

"Fernando, is it? It says here you've been working for many years. Why don't you tell us why you're interested in working here?"

Fernando smiled sweetly and spoke directly to Ms. Clarantia. "I was in the army for many years, and I rose through the ranks quickly. But the higher I went, the further I got from the people I wanted to protect. I want to work somewhere where I can help people directly. Even if I move up here, I'll still be interacting with someone beside other guards." At this, he shot Ms. Clarantia a cheeky wink and turned back to Salvador.

"So you're looking to move up?" Salvador asked, eyeing Fernando over the edge of the clipboard. "You should know that those positions don't open up very often here like they do in the army. It may be many years before you get the opportunity."

Fernando looked back at Ms. Clarantia, who was now watching him with a satisfied smirk. "I've held positions of great honor in the army, and I've worked the meanest jobs. They were all the same to me. Every job is part of my duty as a guard. I just believe that my abilities and work ethic will take me up the ranks here."

Salvador frowned at this. He didn't like the way this man only spoke to Ms. Clarantia. "You say you've held positions of honor. What do you mean by that?"

Fernando looked at Salvador briefly and said, "When I was younger, many years ago, I worked for the Zilonia kingdom. I was one of the best officers there. I was in a team serving with the king's son."

Now this is interesting, Salvador thought. "Which one?"

"Sebastian, the oldest son. But when he disappeared, I retired from the army. I went back to my village and kept the peace there. Now that the Sheevali king's soldiers are all over the place, there's no need for my services anymore. So for me I think it's time to return to the city."

Salvador straightened his papers and nodded at Fernando. "Thank you for your time today. I'll send word when we make a decision."

Fernando stood and dipped into a polite bow, giving Ms. Clarantia a wink. "I appreciate the opportunity and I look forward to hearing from you again."

Ms. Clarantia was mesmerized by Fernando. When he left the room, she wrote a large star beside Fernando's name on her list and turned with a wide grin to Salvador. "Well, I think that settles it. He's perfect. You can finish interviewing if you want, but I think it will be a waste of time at this point. I'm going back to my office to get some work done."

Ms. Clarantia left the room still grinning, positive that Salvador would choose Fernando.

Salvador was relieved that he had an opportunity to interview the other candidates by himself. He wanted to find someone different who would be comparable to Fernando's skills. What Salvador was certain about was that there was no way that he would let this sneaky Fernando on board with his men.

Ms. Gretuala had confided in him that she was afraid. She suspected that trouble was coming their way. He knew she was worried for the girls—he'd seen the look of anguish on her face—but he also had a feeling that it went far beyond that. There was no doubt in his mind that the principal was keeping a secret and one that would bring deadly danger to the school. Salvador knew he would have to be prepared.

THE VIDEO

That night, the wind rattled hard against the windows and the leaves outside had turned a deep orange color. Fiona and Beatrice felt their minds flying as fast as the bitter wind and couldn't sleep no matter how hard they tried. Their thoughts raced over the incident with the video they made. Beatrice tossed and turned in bed before she finally turned toward Fiona.

"Psst! Fiona!" Beatrice whispered. "Are you asleep?"

"Ugh. Of course not! How can I sleep when Nia and her delinquent little friends are hanging that moving picture over us? How did they avoid getting in trouble anyway?"

"Ms. Gretuala must be protecting them. No one else would've gotten away with dumping juice all over you." Beatrice pouted as she said these words.

"Let's follow them around. They've got to be hiding something." Fiona said. "In the meantime, I'll ask my mother if she can help us find that thing of theirs."

Beatrice's brows furrowed. "Are you sure that you want to tell your mother what happened? We could get in huge trouble."

"Yes, I have to," said Fiona confidently. "If this evidence comes up, then even my mother won't be able to help us or herself. She's been so lonely after what happened with my dad; she needs this job. I think I should tell her—the sooner the better. In fact, I'll do it right now."

Beatrice looked at Fiona nervously. "Just don't forget that both of our futures depend on this. You're not the only one getting kicked out if something goes wrong."

Ms. Clarantia was checking the classrooms to be certain that everything was in order for the next day. When Fiona ran up to her, she noticed right away that something was wrong. Her daughter's face was dark and gloomy. Ms. Clarantia took one look and waved her into her office.

"Come on. We'll talk this out." Fiona walked in and sat in the chair opposite her mom's desk. She was shuffling her feet and rubbing her hands.

Ms. Clarantia looked worriedly at her daughter. "What happened? Are you all right?"

Fiona looked down at her hands to avoid her mother's penetrating gaze "Beatrice and I screwed up badly. You're not going to like it."

Ms. Clarantia folded her arms in front of her and glared at Fiona. "What did you do?"

Fiona continued, her voice shaking. "That flooding in the bathroom wasn't an accident. We did it. We wanted to win the best-student award so badly that we decided to cheat. I made the bathroom flood while Beatrice went into the principal's office and stole the magic pen. We wanted to change the score on the board in our favor. Somehow the new girls found out about our plan and they made a moving picture of the entire thing. They threatened to expose us. If the principal had punished them the first time, then we wouldn't be in this stupid situation."

"You did what?" Ms. Clarantia looked confused. "What do you mean moving picture? What does that mean?"

Hot tears threatened to break Fiona's air of indignation. "Those girls have some sort of magic device that shows you the past just as it happened."

"How could you do this?! If Ms. Gretuala finds out about this, you'll be thrown out!" Ms. Clarantia was furious with Fiona and Beatrice, but she knew how to pull herself together.

She took a deep breath, kept her back straight and her face placid, but her voice was cold. "We have to find that thing before anyone else learns about what you did. You girls not only jeopardized your futures, but you also put me in a very difficult situation. Ms. Grenatula trusts me, and if she finds out about what you did and that I knew about it and didn't tell her, she will let me go as well. Do you understand how badly you screwed up? This might ruin us."

Fiona shook in her seat and sniffled as she spoke. "We didn't think it would be like this... We just wanted to win the contest."

"What does this moving picture thing look like?" Ms. Clarantia huffed.

Fiona shook her head. "I'm not really sure. We only saw it for a moment. It was shaped kind of like a box—dark and rectangular with a glass that creates the picture. They called it a camera and said there was a video."

Ms. Clarantia pointed an angry finger at the door. "Go and tell Beatrice to sit tight and stay away from the new girls. I will look for the magical object of which you speak."

When Fiona was gone, Ms. Clarantia sat in thought for a moment. The placidity that she showed to Fiona was gone, replaced by a frown from her chin to her forehead. She knew without a doubt that Fiona and Beatrice were out of line, but Fiona had made a good point. It was very suspicious that Ms. Gretuala didn't punish the new girls for their behavior during dinner the night before, and there was a niggling feeling that she had been kept out of the loop. Perhaps she wasn't trusted now. She felt a shiver of apprehension run up and down her spine. She had to find that thing, and quickly, before anyone else did.

THE RINGS

Jack got home very late after a long first day at work. It was almost midnight, and he was extremely tired. He hadn't expected to start working immediately on his first day. Kace and Orion rushed to speak to him when he returned.

"Did you hear anything at the tavern?" Kace asked.

Jack sighed, his eyes heavy. "More soldiers are coming into the city tomorrow. The Sheevali king knows we're here, and he's looking for you and probably our sisters."

"We'll have to be even more cautious more careful now," Orion said, a concerned wrinkle across his forehead.

Jack, stifling a yawn, added, "There was an officer that came in at the beginning of my shift. He seemed high ranking, and he kept writing in a small notebook. There might be something useful in there. Everyone says he's a regular. Tomorrow I'll try to take a look and see if he wrote anything about us."

Orion walked over to the table and sat down, beckoning the other boys to join him. "We've made some progress with the map." He pointed to a single road leading toward Tiger Mountain. "This is the only road, but it's going to be heavily guarded. There's no way we'll make it if we stick to this route." Orion's finger traced the road until it reached a bridge. "Staying off the road will be easy enough until we get here. This river is too wide and it flows too fast for us to cross safely without using our powers."

Kace looked at Orion. "We'll need to bring a rope with us. I can tie it to the tallest tree on the opposite side of the river. You'll just have to make the tree small enough for me to break it and then big enough that we can use it as a bridge. Once we find a safe path to the mountain, we can come back to get our sisters and free our parents together. We need to be ready for any kind of danger. We can't afford to lead the girls into a trap."

Jack looked at the map that the twins had drafted and then looked curiously at them, trying to discern their meaning. Jack couldn't understand how their abilities could possibly work. "How will you—"

Footsteps could be heard just outside their door. They fell silent and listened for any indication of whom it might be. Then a familiar voice could be heard through the door. "It's just me, your Aunt Greta."

With a sigh of relief, the boys went to greet Greta at the door. She walked in and kissed Kace and Orion on their foreheads. Then she turned to Jack and smiled kindly. "How was your first day at work? Were you able to get any information?"

Jack shrugged, but his voice was quiet. "Everybody is looking for the boys. I hope our sisters are safe at your school."

Greta's heart swelled for Jack. He reminded her of her brother Bruno, always paying close attention to details and looking out for those he cared about. She gave Jack a big hug.

"I promise I will do my best to keep them safe. I will guard them with my life."

"I hate to interrupt," said Orion. "But now that we're all together, we need a strategy to save our family and bring the Zilonian Kingdom to its former power. We're a little short on time, remember? The girls' birthday and the hundred-year spell are just around the corner."

Greta sounded weary as she spoke. "You're right, Orion. Our happy reunion will have to wait. For now, it's all business."

Everyone nodded in agreement as Orion continued. "Our mission is going to be difficult, but it's not like we have much of a choice. We have to try. Kace and I looked at the map—see what we came up with."

Kace opened the map and pointed out to Greta that to cross the river they would have to make their own bridge using their powers. Orion concentrated on the map with a serious look. "We'll pick the most suitable tree and use it as a bridge. Hopefully I can make it as long as we need it."

Greta noticed the look of confusion on Jack's face. "Orion has the power to make things small or big."

"We'll look for a Remuren tree," Orion said. "They only blossom at night, so there won't be any leaves getting in the way."

"It only has leaves at night? That's a bizarre tree," said Jack wrinkling his eyebrows.

"Odd maybe," said Orion, somewhat defensively. "But it has many uses. The sap, for example, is used to make a drink call cafetoori. It gives you all kinds of energy, but it does have some strange side effects."

Jack rolled his eyes. "You mean like talking like a little kid? You should have heard the soldiers at the tavern."

Orion laughed. "Yeah, things like that."

Kace cut in. "We're going to need a very strong rope, one strong enough to pull down a tree—once Orion has shrunk it a bit."

Greta took her belt off and gave it to Kace. "Use my belt. It is as strong as any rope you'll find."

Jack was finally beginning to understand this magic stuff and exclaimed, "Of course, you can change the length of the belt as well!"

A big grin spread across Orion's cheeks. "You got it, brother."

The puzzled look returned to Jack's face. "But how will you be able to bend a tree on the other side of the river?"

Kace patted his chest proudly. "That's my job. I can move and direct any object just with my eyes. Once I have the belt around the tree, Orion shrinks it down enough that we can pull it down at the roots. The key is to do all the steps precisely at the right time. Once it starts to fall, Orion makes it long again—like pulling out a telescope—so that the top part lands on our side of the river. If the timing is bad, the tree drops into the water and we get to watch it float downstream. If all goes well, we find a safe path to the mountain. Once we know the way is safe, we'll bring the girls and save our parents."

"We still need to find the medallion," Greta said, concern running deep in her voice. "While it remains in Grinage's possession, he is a threat to all of us."

"I can get all of the information we need from soldiers in the tavern," Jack said. "When they eat and drink too much, they become very talkative. I'm sure some of them have heard about the medallion."

Greta knew that they were on the right track. She put her hand in her purse and took out a tiny sack filled with little capsules and gave it to Orion. "Please take this. I made a potion for you in case you need to change your appearance."

She took out a small bottle and gave it to Jack. "As I promised, I made a memory potion for you. You use it only if you think you have no other option. All our lives are on the line. Please make sure that the Sheevali king can't read your mind. You are our most vulnerable link when it comes to his powers."

Jack took the bottle from Greta. "Don't worry. I'll use it if I have to."

Greta had another gift for the boys: four plain rings. She handed two of them to Kace and Orion. "These rings used to belong to your parents and Bruno. I have one as well. I want you to have two of them. When the time is right, your sisters will get a ring also. These rings have magical abilities. If you turn one once around your finger, it will become hot and alert us all that you're in trouble. If you turn it twice, it will become cold to tell us you're safe. Unlike our silent communication, which has limited range, with these rings we can communicate at any distance. I will keep my ring on at all times."

Jack was looking at the rings curiously. "If I have to use one of these rings, how it will work with me not having the silent communication ability?"

Greta was impressed by Jack's curiosity. "Smart boy. I'll tell you: When you turn the ring, we will not be able to hear you, but we will be able to read your message. All you have to do is use the finger the ring is on to write a note in the air. We'll see it as if reading a letter." She turned to Kace and Orion. "You can use it that way too, so be mindful of your situation. Jack won't be able to hear you if you speak through your minds."

It was Kace's turn to ask a question he'd needed an answer to for a long time. "Why didn't you ever visit us all these years?"

Greta frowned, a look of sadness crossing her face. "I thought about you every single day, but there are spies ever watching me. I don't know who they are, but I can feel their presence all the time. I couldn't afford to expose you."

Orion looked hopeful. "But you did keep an eye on us, right?

"Yes," said Greta, "That day when Bruno didn't come home, I had Sheevali soldiers watching me closely. Grinage knows that I am your aunt, so he's always paying attention. Even right now before I came here I had to make a few circles around the city to make sure that I wasn't being followed. Eldora is my eyes and ears. All those years that we were apart, she came to me constantly to report how you were doing. I couldn't disclose the place where you were living to anybody because it would put you in danger."

Kace winked at Orion. "We were wondering where that strange cat came from."

Orion piped in. "Eldora's always been very protective of us, and even though she can't speak, we've somehow always known what she wanted us to understand. That makes so much sense now!"

Kace changed the subject to their uncle. "Do you know what happened to Bruno?"

Greta shook her head. "The last I heard from Eldora, he was taken to the Sheevali Castle. I don't know anything beyond that. I don't even know if he is still alive."

"I have one more question, if I may," Jack said. "I have a strange birthmark on my shoulder. Everyone thinks it's a tattoo. We found an object in Bruno's box, and it looks like my birthmark. This might be silly, but I thought you might know something about it."

Kace took the leaf out of the box and showed it to Greta. She compared it to Jack's shoulder. "They look identical. There might be some kind of connection, but honestly I don't have the answer. I will ask my friend Mr. Chapman. You know him from the tavern, Jack. His daughter goes to my school. He knows about magical objects more than me— he collects them. In the meantime, keep this leaf." Greta gave it to Jack.

Greta looked out the window and noticed a thin line of light coming up over the horizon. "The sun will be up soon. I have to leave before anyone notices that I am missing. But before I leave, I have one last gift." She brought out a pot with beautiful blue flowers. She sat the pot in the middle of the window. "If you find that you have to abandon this place, put the pot in the left corner of this window. I'll know that the place has been compromised and you've moved on."

Greta hugged each of the boys and left in a hurry. She had a strong feeling of apprehension, but there was nothing more she could do for them at this time.

MS. CLARANTIA AND THE GARDNER

It was very early in the morning and the wind had died down to a cool breeze, but Lisa and Alexa were already awake when Ms. Clarantia walked into their room. She smiled at them sweetly.

"Girls," she said with her most cheerful tone. "I have a little chore for you today." She held out a stack of papers and handed it to Alexa. "Do you think you can take this to the head guard, Salvador? It's very important that he gets this list soon. He needs to know who to let in the gate today, or some of the other girls won't get to see their families."

Lisa grinned at Ms. Clarantia. "We'd love to help." The girls were very happy for the chance to get to know new people at the school. They took the list and ran to the guards' station.

When Lisa and Alexa left, Ms. Clarantia lingered behind to scan their room with her magical vision. She could see what was inside of the drawers and behind the walls. Using her magic sight, she always knew what was going on in the school, and that made her very valuable. But scanning the girls' room, she found nothing out of the ordinary.

With a scowl she snuck into Nia's room. The room was tiny and clean but it had a big window, which brought in soft light. Nia was already gone, and Ms. Clarantia searched the room as well, again finding nothing. In her frustration, she stomped her foot on the ground. How am I supposed to find this thing? She asked herself. Right when Ms. Clarantia was about to leave, Nia walked in.

Ms. Clarantia was startled, but she quickly regained her composure. "No, nothing here. I was told that there are mice running in the rooms, so I am checking every room looking for signs. Your room looks good." She smiled sweetly at Nia and quickly left.

Out in the hall, Ms. Clarantia breathed a sigh of relief. Nia didn't seem suspicious, but now she had to keep up the pretense and search every corner of the school for signs of mice. Ugh, she said to herself, I don't even know what a video looks like.

On her way back from searching the school, she decided to stop by the garden to see if maybe the video was hidden there. When Ms. Clarantia walked into the conservatory, she saw a man planting beautiful flowers. He was slouched, very scruffy, and untidy, making his appearance displeasing to her. But then he looked up and smiled at Ms. Clarantia.

"Hi, my name is Rufus. I'm the new gardener." The toothless smile split across his wrinkled face. "I have a few roses that I gathered from cleaning the bushes. May I give them to you?"

"Why I... Umm, thank you," Ms. Clarantia stammered.

"You look a bit stressed. You shouldn't mar such a kind face with a gloomy look. The smell of these amazing flowers will perk you right up." Rufus held the flowers out with a flourish.

Ms. Clarantia blushed at the attention. It had been a long time since a man had given her a complement. She sat down next to him and sniffed the roses.

After a moment of enjoying the flowers, she turned to him. "Have you seen a strange-looking box with a glass on one side or any other objects that might be considered unusual? I'm trying to help the new students. They lost a valuable item."

Rufus frowned as he considered if he'd seen it. "I'm sorry, but I've seen nothing of the sort. If I do, I'll bring it to you right away."

Rufus went back to work but then paused as if struck by a sudden thought. "Ms. Gretuala was here earlier to give me my instructions for the day. Maybe she found it. She's coming back later to check my work. I could ask her then?"

Ms. Clarantia shook her head nervously. "No, there's no need for that. The students who lost the item are new, and they have already gotten into trouble once. The principal would be very disappointed in them if she found out that they messed up again."

Rufus nodded gravely. "Ah, it can be hard to adjust to a new environment."

Ms. Clarantia breathed a sigh of relief and spoke with just a little too much enthusiasm. "Yes! We all like these girls, and I really would like to help them, but students can't get in trouble repeatedly without consequences. Ms. Gretuala would be heartbroken if she learned that these new girls were already causing trouble again. She's had a soft spot for them ever since their friends saved her from being robbed. Let's keep it our little secret."

Rufus gave Ms. Clarantia another wide, toothless grin. "Our little secret. I won't bother Ms. Gretuala with this."

When Ms. Clarantia left Rufus he thought, if Ms. Gretuala does have a soft spot for these new girls, there must be more to it. I need to dig a little deeper.

A New Friend

When Lisa and Alexa passed one of the guards' checkpoints, they could hear groaning coming from inside. They came closer and saw a large man lying on the ground. He was holding a hand to the back of his head. There was a thin trickle of blood.

Lisa rushed to his side. "What happened, sir? I'm sorry. I don't know your name."

The guard saw the girls and a look of embarrassment flashed across his face. This was not a position to which he was accustomed.

"My name is Salvador, and I suppose I'm the worst guard here. Something struck my head while I was doing my regular checks and everything went black. I don't know how long I was unconscious." He tried to push himself to his feet, but fell back down, clasping his head tighter. "Augh! My head hurts like crazy and I think I might throw up!"

Lisa closed her eyes and put her arms around Salvador's head, her magic closing his wound and easing his pain. When she opened her eyes again, Salvador was staring at her in shock.

"How'd you do that?" he asked, gingerly touching his head.

"It's my magic power. Please don't tell anyone though. We're not exactly supposed to use our powers in school, and I want to stay out of trouble"

Salvador stood up and shook his head. "You can count on me anytime you need my help. After what you did just now, please know that you have a friend here."

Alexa laughed in delight. "We don't have many friends here. It's so nice to meet you! As your friends, we could help find out what really happened to you. Someone is obviously trying to hurt you, since it doesn't look like anything fell down accidentally."

Salvador nodded, mainly to himself. This little girl might have a point, he thought. He looked around the room. Nothing seemed out of place. Folding his heavy arms across his broad chest, he said, "It's possible. My schedule is always the same, so it would be easy to track me. Every night I light the lanterns and every morning I put them out. The same goes for the rest of the guards. They make regular checks of the grounds every two hours to make sure everything is all right. I suppose we're too predictable. I even thought I heard quiet steps behind me earlier, but I assumed it was the black-and-white cat I sometimes see walking around."

Lisa and Alexa looked at each other and giggled. "It must be Eldora," Alexa thought to Lisa. "But I doubt that he could hear her steps."

"If you don't mind," said Lisa. "We'll stop by this evening to do your routine check with you. I think we can sneak out after curfew to help."

Alexa burst with excitement. "I can help you light the lanterns!"

Salvador looked at her quizzically. "It's tricky to get to them, but I'll show you how it's done."

Alexa laughed. "You'll be surprised to find that I'm a very quick learner."

When the girls were about to leave, Alexa heard a noise coming from the wall. She squinted her eyes suspiciously and, turning to Lisa and Salvador, dropped her voice to a whisper. "I think someone is listening to us. Are there any secret compartments around here where someone can hide?"

Salvador nodded. "I've heard there may be a tunnel behind the walls, but I don't know where the doors are. They are hidden from sight."

"Salvador, I think you're in danger here," Lisa said, her eyes shifting between the guard and the wall nervously. "Someone is clearly after you."

Alexa winked at both of them and pointed to herself. "The good thing is, this someone knows you're not alone. We'll help you."

THE CAFE OWNER

In the morning, Jack got up early. Greta had stayed very late, and he could feel the sleep in his eyes as he looked out the window and saw the leaves on the plants turning a vibrant green. Knowing the signs as he now did, he thought, it's going to be a nice, bright day.

As he was about to leave for work, Kace stopped him and placed one of the rings from Aunt Greta in his hand. "We want you to have it. Orion and I have ours, and you should have one of your own. You do remember how it works?"

Jack yawned and rubbed his eyes with the back of his hand. "Yep, it's a piece of cake. I've handled more sophisticated devices than this one." He put it in his pocket and added, "It should stay there—jewelry's for girls."

Orion smiled at Jack. "Come on. Just put it on, macho boy. If you lose it we don't have a replacement. Besides, what's with that earing if jewelry is for girls?"

Jack rummaged through his pocket and took the ring out. "Fine, I'll do it so you feel at ease. Now you should get some rest. You have a long night ahead of you."

Jack left the house in a hurry. He was running late. He considered his options and realized that the only way that he would make it in time was if he passed by the café where Elsa worked. Jack looked back at the cottage and yawned again. I know we promised not to, but just this once will be fine. Elsa and her boss won't be looking for one boy who's not even a twin.

When Jack ran by, Bruce was standing outside of his café. Bruce called Elsa out and pointed at Jack's retreating figure. "Is this one of the boys that we saw yesterday? I thought you said they weren't up to anything, but it's a little early for a tourist to be out."

Elsa looked hard at Jack's back. "It might be one of them. I talked to the brothers yesterday, and they said that they were just visitors. They were pretty convincing. They're new in town. I don't think that they're the twins that the Sheevali king is looking for. If they were the twins, they wouldn't go out in the middle of the day knowing that everybody is looking for them and that boy wouldn't walk by your café so openly knowing you're suspicious."

Bruce narrowed his eyes and gave a spiteful frown. "Maybe so, but something about them still rubs me the wrong way. I shouldn't have left an important task like that up to you, but my wife is always getting herself into accidents in the kitchen."

He looked back at the house where he'd seen Jack emerge and connected it with the twins. He turned to Elsa. "Keep an eye on that place for me. Who knows, maybe your tourists will show up there as well."

BELLA'S BIRTHDAY

Queen Antoinette was in her opulent quarters. No expense was spared. The entire suite was extremely well crafted and full of exotic decorations. Adjacent to the luxurious room was the queen's magic pool given to her as a wedding present from her husband. The water didn't just cleanse the body, but it made it invisible to the eyes, preserved youthfulness, and gave off a rejuvenating energy. Every day the queen took her bath there.

The queen, Bella's mother, was lavishing in her magical swimming pool, letting her head float at the surface while her body was made invisible beneath the magic water. Her dazzling blue eyes stood out in contrast to her black hair, peach-colored skin and light-hued lips. Bella sat on a bench beside the pool painting her new china set.

After her run-in with Antuan, Bella found it hard to choose a theme for her work. She hated to admit it, but his comments about her art had stung in a way she didn't think possible. Her father would always admire her work and give her a lot of complements. Now she was questioning her talent.

The princess looked up to see a tall and lean servant woman polishing the crystal in the queen's bedroom. She thought about how hard Victoria worked and how much the woman meant to her. Antoinette's voice broke into her thoughts. "Your birthday is right around the corner. What would you like for a present? I'm certain there's something delightfully lavish that I can talk your father into buying for you."

Bella answered quickly to keep her mother from suggesting something ridiculous. "To cancel the engagement announcement to Antuan."

The queen let out a tinkling giggle. "I'm afraid that I can't do that. On my seventeenth birthday, your father and I announced our engagement. You, my dear, are going to be eighteen soon, and it's time for you to grow up."

The queen's eyes sparkled with delight. "I know what we'll do—we'll have an academy competition between the cadets of the kingdom. This way, you will see Antuan differently. You will see him as a man and not as a silly little boy. Antuan is one of the best students in the kingdom—maybe even the best. I think this event will help you change your mind about him."

The queen let out a laugh and slid beneath the surface of the water, becoming completely invisible and free from her daughter's response.

Bella rolled her eyes. Sometimes her mother acted just like a child herself. Why should she expect differently from Bella?

Bella looked up from the surface of the water just in time to see Victoria finishing up with the last crystal on the lamp there by the open window. She watched helplessly as Victoria turned and accidentally bumped the lamp—the queen's favorite—from the ledge. It fell from the window and shattered upon the ground below. Bella had seen her mother severely punish other servants for a lot less. Victoria shook with terror.

Bella hurried to the window, turning herself into the lamp just in time for the queen to surface. Antoinette looked around the room then turned to Victoria. "Where is Isabella?"

Stunned, Victoria simply shook her head and answered nervously, "She, ah, just left. Someone was calling her name."

The door shut quickly, and Victoria knew the queen had left. When it was clear that it was safe, Bella switched herself back to normal and took Victoria's hand. "Don't worry, I'll tell my mom that I accidentally broke the lamp. She won't punish me the way she does her servants."

Victoria was dumbfounded by Bella's generosity. She wrapped Bella in a tight hug and whispered in her ear. "I am forever in your debt."

Bella smiled and held Victoria at arm's length. "No need, I'm glad that I could help you. You are always so honest with me. I trust you. You must know how very rare that is here in the castle. Now go and quickly sweep up those crystals before somebody notices them."

Victoria grabbed the broom and a sack and ran out.

ON THE RUN

Orion looked out the window and noticed Sheevali soldiers going door to door. He cracked the window a tiny bit and caught the edge of the soldiers' conversation. His heart sank when he heard the word "twins" pass between them. It was obvious that they were searching for the boys.

Orion shut the window quickly and called out to Kace in an anxious whisper. "We need to leave now. It's only a matter of time before the soldiers find us here."

Kace joined Orion at the window and peeked out at the street. He saw the soldiers walk into a house a block away from them. "As soon as they go inside the next house, we need to get out of here and start heading for Tiger Mountain. It has to be separately though. You leave first. When the soldiers go into the following house, I'll leave too. Let's meet at the well next to the abandoned farm."

Orion watched the soldiers intently. As soon as the soldiers went across the street and entered another door, he ran out of the cottage, taking Alexa's scarf with him to cover his face. He was able to pass by the café unnoticed, taking advantage of a mutt that was distracting the patrons by barking furiously at Alexa's cat. Bruce was trying to shoo Eldora away from his patio roof, but the cat just kept hissing to drive the pooch even crazier. Everyone watched with glee as Bruce began climbing up after Eldora.

When his climbing didn't work, Bruce ran inside of the café, carrying a long-handled broom with him. He swiped at Eldora with the rough bristles. With a final hiss, the cat jumped off the gutter she was sitting on and ran away.

Kace smirked as he watched the scene. Huh, smart cat, he thought. Eldora had given them time to escape. But he tarried too long. By the time he looked away from the scene at the café, the soldiers were already at the next door. Their cottage was next. Trying his best to look like a man running errands, he grabbed a sack and flung it across his shoulders before walking out the door.

As he did, the café owner spotted him and called to his wife, Angelina. "You see that boy over there? I'm almost certain that's who those soldiers are looking for. I'll follow him and try to catch him. You warn the guards."

Kace noticed Bruce pointing at him and broke into a run, heading straight into the bakery from the day before. Taking the back door, he saw a horse with a wagon of hay in the alley. He leapt inside and covered himself with straw. He tried to stay perfectly still as a slouching gentleman came out of the back door, got up onto the wagon, and drove it away.

Bruce ran into the bakery after Kace, checking the café, the bathroom, and finally the back door. But when Bruce made it outside, it was too late. No one was there. All he could see was a carriage turning the corner.

Feeling dejected, Bruce walked back to his own café. He spotted his wife chatting with Officer Seagull.

"The twins live in that house." Angelina pointed at the shack across from their café. "We just saw one try to sneak out. My husband went after him." Both the officer and Angelina looked at Bruce expectantly.

Bruce shook his head sadly. "I tried to follow him but I lost him. I think he might have noticed me. He disappeared before I could catch up with him."

Officer Seagull pulled out his black notebook. "Do you think you could describe what they look like?"

Bruce shook his head again. "I haven't seen them closely enough. My waitress, Elsa, spoke to them the other day. She could probably give you a description."

Officer Seagull put his notebook back into the pocket of his coat. "Have the girl meet me at the tavern down the road. I'll speak with her there—and don't keep me waiting." He barked at them.

A NOTE FROM THE SPY

Grinage was standing next to the open window and gazing out at the western mountains when Ferocious landed on the window pane with a letter tied to its leg. Upon opening the letter, Grinage realized that it was from a spy that Sebastian sent into the girls' school a few years ago. He sighed grumpily as he unrolled the paper. This spy had never delivered the way Sebastian had promised. She was a disappointment from the start. Grinage's brows furrowed as he read.

Majesty,

I'm writing to inform you that the plan to get rid of Officer Salvador, the head of security at the Fairyton Institute, has failed. I'd hoped to compromise his abilities before the leaders of the school. I attacked him and left him unconscious. However, two new girls have interfered. One of them has healing powers. She doesn't use any herbs or potions. She can heal with her hands. Both girls stay close to the guard, suspecting he is in danger. I would like to have your permission to stay low for a while to avoid being compromised. I will concentrate my efforts on these two mysterious girls. Supposedly they are just friends, but there seems to be a closer connection. I will get to the bottom of it.

Always at your service, 1 1 3

The king threw the letter down in disgust. "Again this worthless spy has failed me!" He turned on the nearest servant. "Bring Sebastian in here!"

Sebastian marched in almost immediately, concern splashed clearly across his rugged features. With his hand trembling with rage, Grinage pointed down at the letter. "This spy is useless. I want this brainless insect out! I have too many servants that are better at their job than this tiny worm!"

Sebastian bent down to pick up the soiled letter. Slowly and calmly he read it through, taking in every word. After a moment's thought, he cleared his throat and spoke clearly but tentatively. "If I may, Your Majesty, I think we should keep the spy there for a little bit longer. She has been there for a long time, and she is the only one who can blend in without being suspected. She may not have delivered any results yet, but she is in the safest position there. Let's see what she can find out about these mysterious girls. We do not want to start a war and bring chaos to a group of children if there is nothing special about those girls. Let's concentrate on finding the twin boys. They will lead us to their sisters. We know that they are in the city, and we need to find them."

Grinage's anger dissipated. Sebastian was right, of course. Grinage liked that his general could always find a way to take advantage of any situation, no matter how complex. He let out a sigh and nodded in agreement.

"You're right, my friend. I should have just trusted your decision. I'll agree to leave her in the school for now, but all of her communication must come through you now. Greta will do what she can to undermine me, and we can't let that stand. You know your sister better than anyone else, and I'm counting on you. I'm losing my patience. If I don't see results soon, I will bring my anger upon her precious school."

AMISON

As the evening darkness grew, the girls ran to meet Salvador as promised. Despite his normally stern demeanor, he was elated at the thought of teaching them to light the lanterns. He was looking all around the guardhouse for the lighting wand, but he couldn't find it.

While he searched, he found that he was whistling a cheerful tune to himself, something he hadn't felt like doing in years. He imagined the delight on the girls' faces as he sent bright colorful balls of fire spiraling out of the long lighting wand, each bursting into a fireworks display to light the lanterns.

Not finding the wand in the guardhouse, Salvador was about to leave to search the storage shed when the lantern in the first tower burst into light. He turned to see Alexa and Lisa in a fit of laughter and surrounded by a swarm of tiny fireflies.

Salvador felt his jaw go slack. "How could this be?"

The girls spotted Salvador staring at them and waved him over. "Where are the other lights?" Alexa called. "I want to get every single one!"

Salvador lifted a shaking finger and pointed toward the tip of the next tower. Alexa shot a quick fireball at the lantern, lighting it up in a burst of flame. In no time, all of the lights were on.

Salvador took his hat off, touched his head with awe, and muttered a quiet blessing. "That was amazing. How did you—"

"Alexa? Lisa? Are you girls out here?" It was Ms. Gretuala running across the grounds toward them.

Alexa and Lisa looked at each other frantically. "She knows we snuck out!" Lisa said.

"We better go right away then. She'll only get more upset if she can't find us." The girls took off in her direction. When they reached Ms. Gretuala, the woman was gasping for breath.

"Girls, come with me. I need your help." Her voice shook with worry.

Without question, Lisa and Alexa followed Ms. Gretuala. She led them deep into the school building into the magical animal room where she locked the door behind them. Inside was a private universe of colors and patterns. A soft, color-changing light seemed to emanate from the room itself, bathing everything in a warm glow. The girls felt giddy taking in all the wonders that the room had to offer. All around were strange and exotic animals that neither of the girls had ever seen or heard of before, each with its own unique power.

But Greta passed through the room as if none of the wonder could touch her. She headed directly to a birdhouse where a tiny golden bird with a silver crown laid unconscious.

"It's Amison. I found him like this. Please, see if you can heal him, Lisa? I know about your powers."

Lisa approached the bird and put her hand on top of his head. She took Amison gently into her hands and raised the limp figure up to her lips, granting him a light kiss. The bird's eyes fluttered open and he let out a cheerful tweet. Amison hopped around Lisa's hand happily and up onto Lisa's shoulder. Suddenly both Lisa and Amison became invisible.

"Lisa! You're gone!" Alexa exclaimed.

With a laugh, Lisa gingerly pulled Amison from her shoulder, making herself visible again, and gave him back to Ms. Gretuala, who watched the whole scene wide-eyed.

"I knew about your ability, but it certainly looks like a miracle in person." Greta patted the little golden bird and brought him up to her cheek, feeling the softness of his feathers. "I have to let you go now, my dear Amison. Someone tried to hurt you, and if they know that you are alive they will be back."

She opened a small window and let the bird out.

Lisa stood admiring Ms. Gretuala's kind heart for a moment before a thought struck her. "How did you know that I have the power of healing?"

For a moment, Greta stared at Lisa with a wild look in her eyes. But then her expression softened. Greta knew that it was time to tell the girls the truth. "Because I am your aunt and I know all of your powers. I've been helping your brothers prepare to find your parents so you four can save the kingdom from the Sheevalis."

Lisa gulped nervously, "You mean our birth parents are somewhere here?"

Alexa opened her mouth in shock. "They're alive?"

"Yes. I promise to tell you all about it later in a safer environment." Greta looked around, making sure that no one was listening to them, and all three of them slowly headed to the door. The girls desperately wanted to know all about their parents, and it intrigued them. How could they possibly save their parents and the entire Zilonia Kingdom? However, but this was not the time or place for conversation.

As they were walking, Greta continued to speak, "I knew you were telling the truth about Fiona and Beatrice because of my own powers. I can always tell if words are true or false."

Alexa hopped up and down with joy. "Now it makes sense! When you said that you believed us about Fiona and Beatrice, without any kind of punishment, we thought that it might've been because you're our aunt."

"Also," Lisa chimed in. "We knew that our brothers wouldn't bring us here unless they were positive that they could trust someone to watch over us."

Greta enveloped both girls in a tight hug. "You are such smart girls!" She pulled away to look sternly into their eyes. "We need to keep this a strict secret. If anyone learns the truth, we'll all be in deep danger. The Sheevali king has his eyes and ears everywhere, including this school, so you must be very careful."

OUT OF THE CITY

As soon as the carriage left the city, Kace jumped off the wagon and ran toward the forest. The rustling of hay alerted the driver, and he turned around just in time to see Kace speeding away into the woods. He raised his fist into the air and shouted after Kace.

"You won't get away with this! The soldiers will be on your blasted tail before you're halfway through the woods!"

Kace could hear the man's angry shouts as he ran hard and breathless into the forest, trying to put as much distance between himself and the carriage driver as possible. He had to catch up with Orion quickly.

Orion waited nervously in front of the farm on the outskirts of the city. It had been too long and Kace had not yet arrived.

Finally, in the distance, Orion saw a figure running toward him. He knew those curly golden locks anywhere; it was Kace. A wave of relief washed away his fears.

When Kace approached Orion, he was gasping for breath. He leaned hard against the fence surrounding the farm and gulped air into his aching lungs. After several seconds, he said, "The café owner spotted me. I had to run away and hide in the back of a wagon until the driver got out of town. The driver saw me though. He turned back toward the city. I'm certain he's going to tell the soldiers about me."

"I guess we'll have to use this then." Orion pulled out the powder Greta had given him and handed a capsule to Kace. "We need to change our appearance in case anyone got a good look at us."

The brothers shook the powder all over their heads, and their beautiful sun stained, curly hair turned dark and slick with spikes standing straight and tall. The boys looked at each other and laughed.

"Aunt Greta must have added something extra to make our hair so fancy!" Kace exclaimed.

Newly changed, the brothers hurried toward the mountains. As they walked deeper into the forest, they set the traps that Bruno had taught them to make. Anyone setting foot upon one would send out a bear's roar that could be heard for miles.

ENDANGERED

When the wagon driver reached the tavern, he walked inside and saw Officer Seagull sitting at a table with a young woman. He was looking at the sketch that he had made from Elsa's description. It showed two moonfaced boys, identical in looks. They were short and stout, with beady brown eyes, round turned-up noses like a pig's, and matching mops of curly blonde hair.

As the driver approached Officer Seagull, he recognized the young woman as Elsa right away. He saw her often when he delivered milk to the café where she worked. "Elsa, my dear, I hope you're not wrapped up in this fugitive business?"

Elsa looked up from the table and gave the man a weak smile. "It's good to see you, Bart. We don't run into each other here very often. Mr. Bruce thinks I might've been a witness, but I'm not so sure."

Bart took his hat off and nodded at Officer Seagull. "Begging your pardon, since I don't mean to interrupt, but I saw something that might help with your search. Just as I brought my wagon out of the city, a boy jumped out from the back and ran toward the mountains. He must've been hiding there awhile. I never saw him climb in."

Officer Seagull pointed at the sketch made from Elsa's description. "Did he look anything like this?"

Bart shook his head. "I didn't see his face, but he was tall, athletic, and he had bright-white hair. Aside from the hair color, these boys look nothing like the boy I saw."

The officer squinted his already narrow eyes at Bart. "And you're sure he was alone?"

Bart gave what he hoped was a convincing nod. "Yes, sir, positive."

"Very well then," said Officer Seagull. "This incident probably isn't related to the twins, but show us which way that young man went. We'll check it out."

Officer Seagull began standing up, and Elsa saw her chance to get away. "Excuse me, sir, but is there anything more you need from me?"

Officer Seagull looked at her as if he'd already forgotten about her. "No. I have everything I need from you."

Elsa left the table and let Bart take her seat. She spotted Jack emerging from the kitchen and signaled for him to join her behind the tavern. Jack frowned but he followed.

When they were outside Elsa turned around and looked at Jack. "I recognize you. You're a friend of the twins. I saw all of you that day at the bakery."

"What do you want from me?" Jack snarled. "Are you out for the king's reward like everyone else?"

"I want nothing!" Elsa exclaimed. "I just wanted to let you know that the soldiers are looking for your friends. I had to give them a description of the twins because the café owner made me, but I gave them the wrong description. I don't want those boys captured any more than you do.

They're just tourists after all, and they never did anything to me that wasn't plain nice. That blasted milkman talking to Officer Seagull is going to undo everything though. He's giving the correct description. I think one of your friends was hiding in his wagon and ran off toward the mountains once they were out of the city. You need to warn your friends in case they are in trouble. I can't do any more for them."

Jack looked at Elsa in shock. When he opened his mouth to speak, his voice came out shaky and uncertainly. "Thank you. I'm sorry for my rudeness before, it's just that my friends are always getting accused. I won't forget your kindness."

Elsa blushed, noticing the attractive lines of Jack's face. "It was nothing. I— I have to go!" She turned and ran from the alley, trying to hide her embarrassment.

When Elsa was gone, Jack looked at the ring and turned it once to let the boys know that they had been compromised and that the soldiers were after them. With his ring finger out, Jack wrote a message into the air as Greta had instructed him.

"You are compromised. Soldiers are after you." And he darted back into the tavern to avoid rousing suspicion.

THE BLACK BOOK

When Jack returned from the alley, Mr. Chapman waved him into his office. Jack walked in without a word and watched with curiosity as the man reached into a drawer in his desk and took out a small wooden box. He handed it to Jack. "Go ahead and open it."

When Jack opened the box he saw a gold stud earring nestled inside. "Ms. Gretuala asked me to look after you and help if you were to need anything," Mr. Chapman continued. "I collect magical objects; I think you'll find this one very handy. I see the way Officer Seagull looks at you. He's on to something. This earring will open any lock. If you get captured, all you need to do is insert it into the keyhole of whatever lock binds you. Now go back to work before he notices how long you've been gone."

Jack gulped and traded his own earring with Mr. Chapman's gift. "Thank you, sir."

When Jack emerged from the kitchen again, he saw soldiers sitting everywhere, some even scattered about the floor. The tavern was a mass of loud, singing men with voices like children. Only Officer Seagull's table had a ring of space around it. His men gave him wide berth. Jack walked up to Officer Seagull's table and saw him hunched over Elsa's sketch in concentration. Noticing Jack's presence, he looked up and gave a sneering smile. "It's nice to see you return. I thought for sure that you'd forgotten about me."

Jack shivered under the man's cold stare, but he clamped his teeth tight and offered a toothy smile. "Just a little work in the back. I'm here now. What would you like to order, sir?"

Seagull found himself impressed by the way Jack handled the pressing, but he couldn't help testing the boy further. He turned back to the sketches in front of him and appeared disinterested. "The same as yesterday."

As Jack wrote out Officer Seagull's order, he noticed that the black book was on the table. He turned and left, hearing the officer command a few of his soldiers to follow the milkman and see if they could find the young fugitive who was hiding in his wagon. He told his men that he would meet them after he finished eating his lunch.

Jack scurried into the kitchen, returning a few moments later with a steaming bowl of lamb stew. As he carried the hot bowl, he navigated through the mass of patrons. He was doing well when, coming up to the officer's table, he tripped over the leg of a soldier who had sprawled out on the floor, spilling the entire contents of the bowl all over Officer Seagull.

All noise in the tavern suddenly ceased, the patrons holding their breath to see what would happen to Jack.

Jack stared wide eyed, mouth agape, the broth dripping from Officer Seagull—lumps of lamb and potato rolling off of his formerly pristine uniform.

It looked as if Officer Seagull might speak, but Mr. Chapman swooped in between them and hustled the officer away toward the bathroom. "My deepest apologies, sir. I'll do everything I can to make sure that boy is punished for his idiocy."

Without thinking, Jack grabbed the black book and ran into Mr. Chapman's office. He looked through the book and saw that Officer Seagull was screening anyone who possibly had a magical power. It became clear that he was a recruiter for the Sheevali king's army. Each name in Seagull's book included a sketch and a list of their magical skills.

Jack recognized Bruno's name right away. This was proof that Bruno had been taken by the Sheevali king. When Jack returned, Officer Seagull was looking everywhere for his black book. Jack bent down and pretended to pick the book up from the ground. "Sir, is this what you're looking for?"

Officer Seagull turned on Jack and snarled at him. "Did you take it?"

Jack looked hurt. "No, of course not. It must have fallen in the corner when I accidentally spilled the stew on you. I am very sorry about that, sir."

Officer Seagull pointed an angry finger at Jack. "There's something off about you, boy. I can feel it. I can't read you, but I know that you're hiding something. I'm taking you to the Sheevali king. He'll be able to find out if you're hiding a magical skill or keeping a secret."

Hoping to buy more time, Jack burst out, "Can I at least get my things?"

Officer Seagull smirked and fixed Jack with a cold stare. "No. Take him."

Jack sucked in his breath and backed away from Officer Seagull while he turned his ring once again and quickly wrote out the message behind his back with his finger. "In trouble. Captured."

DISASTER

Kace felt his ring grow hot. A line of gold lettering circled around in front of them.

"You are compromised. Soldiers are after you."

A few minutes later, a second message appeared. "In trouble. Captured."

Kace looked at Orion with a worried expression. "We need to split up. They're only looking for one of us. If they find us together, it will be even more suspicious. We have to keep our force-field powers a secret in case one of us gets captured. If we can keep that power secret, hopefully we won't be recognized with this new look."

Orion split away from Kace, taking a steep path while Kace followed the original path through the valley and toward the river. Behind them, a booming roar sounded, signaling that the soldiers were getting close.

Orion was going up the mountain as fast as he could. When he reached a flat spot, he found a hiding place where he could look down on Kace. From his vantage point, Orion could see the soldiers surrounding his brother.

Using his power, Kace flung rocks at the soldiers as he ran and tore trees from the ground by the roots to block their path. But there were too many soldiers for Kace to handle alone. One soldier managed to grab Kace, holding him down until another could tie his hands. Kace was hauled roughly to his feet and escorted back to the road.

Orion watched it all, his anger and frustration building. When the soldiers grabbed Kace and dragged him away, he crept through the forest after them. When he came to the bottom of the hill, he cupped his hands around his mouth and let out a high coyote howl to signal to Kace. At that moment, Officer Seagull arrived on the road just outside of the woods.

A runner had been sent ahead to deliver the news about Kace. He stood at attention while he spoke to Officer Seagull. "Sir, we found a young man, but he doesn't fit the description. This boy has dark hair."

Officer Seagull wasn't satisfied. "I want to speak with him personally. I will leave nothing to chance. He could be hiding something."

Just then, a second coyote howl reached his ears, raising his suspicions. It was unlike a single coyote to follow soldiers in the middle of the day. He looked in the direction the sound had come from and grinned. "That's no animal. Go check it out."

Back in the woods, Orion realized his mistake and tried to hide but there were too many men. He found himself surrounded. Immediately he shrank their spears and knives, leaving the soldiers with useless children's toys. But these were men trained in combat and they continued to advance weaponless.

Two soldiers came at Orion at once. He flicked his eyes at them, and their pants shrank on their bodies, bursting at the seams. While the soldiers were distracted, Orion swung at them, laying them flat.

But this small victory made him cocky, and instead of running he turned to laugh at the soldiers. "I have more power in me than all of you combined. You're no match for me!"

All of a sudden Orion felt a vice-like grip on the back of his neck. The low, growling laugh of Officer Seagull reached his ears. "Got you!"

Back at the road, his catch in tow, Officer Seagull looked at the brothers and compared them to the sketch Elsa had given him. They looked nothing like what she had described, but their skills were useful enough. He turned and ordered his men. "Take them back to the kingdom. The king will decide what to do with them."

TERRIBLE NEWS

Greta was in the middle of a meeting when her ring grew extremely hot. A look of pain flashed over her face. She knew that the boys were in trouble.

"Is everything all right, Ms. Gretuala?" The teacher seated beside her looked concerned.

Ms. Gretuala tried to give her most reassuring smile. "Everything is fine. I'm just not feeling well. Maybe we should adjourn for today and meet again tomorrow." As she tried to leave, Ms. Sofia approached her.

"Ms. Gretuala, I just received a complaint about the two new girls. Someone spotted them using their powers."

"I'll look into it personally," Greta said. "But for now I need to go." Greta rushed out of the meeting and darted into her office.

During the last hour, her ring had grown hot twice. Her worst fears had been realized: the twins and Jack were captured, and it was certain that they'd face King Grinage now. Their plan would be compromised if Jack didn't have the chance to take the memory potion. They were in terrible trouble.

Greta grabbed her purse and rushed out of the school, calling for her carriage as she went. She asked the carriage driver to take her to Mr. Chapman's tavern. She had to know what had happened.

When they arrived, she looked around to make sure that nobody was following her and darted into the building.

Nia's father was in the kitchen when Greta walked in. He saw her and waved her into his office. She followed, trying to keep her agitation from showing. But once they were alone, her resolve broke.

"They took him. I'm so sorry, Greta. There was nothing I could do. Officer Seagull thinks he's hiding an ability."

"He knows everything," Greta wailed. "I gave him a memory potion, but what if he doesn't have a chance to take it?"

Mr. Chapman patted her on the shoulder. "Jack is a very bright boy. He'll find a way out. I gave him a magic earring that he can use as a key to open any door or lock. I'm sure he'll use it wisely."

Greta wasn't convinced, "There's something about that boy that I just can't put my finger on. I can feel that he belongs to us, but there is a secret to him. He has a birthmark on his shoulder in the shape of a leaf—the same as a crystal the boys found in Bruno's cottage. Do you know anything about the leaf? There must be some kind of connection."

Mr. Chapman opened his safe and took out a tattered old book, its pages yellowed and the plain leather cover curling with age. He flipped through it until he came to a place where a single page had been torn out. "Last time I saw Bruno, he asked me if he could take a look at this book. When I gave it to him, all of the pages were intact. He may have taken this page."

Greta looked at the torn remainder of the page. "What's this book about?"

"It's about activating power in people who are only partially of royal blood."

"It doesn't make any sense. What would Bruno need with a page from that book? He didn't have any children, and I know of no one in our family who would need it. My goodness! I'm so upset that I can't even think clearly."

Mr. Chapman shook his head. "I have to tell you more unpleasant news, Greta. The Sheevali soldiers are after the twins as we speak. A milkman discovered one of them hiding in his wagon and came back to the city to tell Officer Seagull. They went after him."

Greta wiped her tears and shook her head. Her voice was barely above a whisper. "They're not just after one. I just got the message that both of the brothers were captured by the Sheevali soldiers."

Greta embraced her old friend. "I have to go. If the king realizes who they are, he'll be coming for me next and I need to be ready for him."

UNDERCOVER

As much as magic was forbidden in the school without instructor supervision, the girls practiced every moment they were alone. After only a few days they were able to control the strength of their shield, activating it at will. They even learned to control the direction of their shield, surrounding themselves with a dome or pointing it to different places in the room. But they soon found that the tiny space was too confining, so they took their practice into the conservatory.

Alexa discovered that if she blew on a fireball hard enough, she could aim it more accurately or even extinguish it if she wanted. It was a remarkable finding. All she had to do was learn to control the force of her breath.

The garden was gigantic and lushly decorated with outlandish and bizarrely shaped shrubs and plants. Practicing throwing her fireballs at a distance and putting them out before they reached their target, Alexa held out her hand within which was cupped a small pile of foam. Her fireflies ignited it, and with all of her strength she threw it as far as she could. But just as she let it go, she let out a great sneeze and sent it sailing into a rosebush.

A yelp rang out from the bush, startling the girls. They ran to see what had happened and found the gardener crouched in the dirt, rubbing his back.

"Are you okay, sir?" Lisa said, rushing to his side. "We didn't mean to hurt you at all." She put her hands on his back and held them there until the pain went away.

The gardener looked at her gratefully. "Thank you. How did you do that?"

Lisa looked at him shyly. "We're so very sorry."

Rufus smiled at her sweetly. "My name is Rufus, and I'm the new gardener. What you just did was very impressive." He turned his focus to Alexa. "You should be more careful, young lady. You possess very powerful magic, and you need to learn the responsibility that comes with it."

Alexa looked frightened and dejected. She'd never hit anyone with her fireballs before, and she was suddenly grateful that her powers were still weak.

Rufus noticed the awkwardness in the two girls and tried to put them at ease. "Well, no one was truly hurt in any case. But what are you doing here?"

Alexa, trying not to look too guilty, said, "We wanted to practice our powers in a place where we would have more space. Our room is too small."

A broad grin grew across Rufus's face. "It's all right. You can do it here, and if I see somebody coming I'll let you know."

"You won't turn us in to Ms. Clarantia?" asked Lisa.

Rufus shook his head. "I don't see how practicing will harm anyone." The girls were surprised and grateful.

"Thank you!" Alexa grinned. "We'll try to keep it down."

Rufus went back to working on the roses while watching the girls from the corner of his eye.

Alexa continued to practice her fireballs while Lisa watched.

Any of the girls in the school could be the twins King Grinage was searching for, Rufus thought to himself, but these two seemed like they might have potential. All Rufus had left to do was see if they could create a force field.

Lisa sat next to Rufus and admired the flowers. Rufus picked two of the most beautiful roses and gave them to her. "One is for you, and the other one is for your friend."

Lisa put her nose to one of the roses and gasped. "I've never smelled anything like this before. Roses smell different where I'm from."

Rufus stopped working and looked at Lisa curiously. "Where are you from?"

Lisa's face flushed red, but she recovered quickly. "I'm from a small village in the woods. We don't have roses there, not real ones. Only small forest flowers that we call small roses."

Rufus's suspicions grew. He looked up at the back door and spotted a large metal lid. "I have an idea."

He walked over to the lid and picked it up, holding it out for Alexa to see. "Your fireballs are weak because you don't believe in your powers. You need a real target. Try to throw a ball at this metal lid. I'll hold it up as a shield." And see if you have any other powers, he thought. When Alexa threw the fireball, Rufus planned to drop the shield to see if the girls would create a force field around him to prevent his being hurt.

Alexa hesitated. "What if I hit you again? I don't want to cause you any harm."

Rufus smiled sweetly at Alexa. "The only way for you to learn to control the strength of your power is if you have a real target to concentrate on. Your fireballs aren't strong enough to hurt anybody yet, not much."

"You have a great eye, Alexa," Lisa encouraged. "And you aim very well when you're not sneezing!"

Finally Alexa nodded and held back her arm to throw her first fireball. Just then, Ms. Clarantia walked in and gave the girls a stern look. "What are you doing here?"

Rufus rushed up to Ms. Clarantia, brandishing three amazingly gorgeous roses. "I'm so sorry, but it was my fault. I asked the girls to help me with these pots. I put them in different places and forgot where they were originally. They all look the same to me. When the girls offered their help, I was very grateful."

Ms. Clarantia frowned at Rufus, distrust showing on her face. "Girls, it is past curfew. Go back to your room immediately."

Ms. Clarantia watched them leave before sending Rufus another suspicious glance. She'd have to watch him she realized; there was something rather unpleasant about him.

THE CAT'S TRUE FACE

When Greta neared the cottage where the boys were staying she saw the flower pot in the left corner of the window. She ached to go inside, but she knew the place had been compromised. Scanning the area, she saw two soldiers sitting in the café and watching the house. Acting as casually as possible, she continued past the cottage and toward a nearby park. She found a secluded bench and sat down, holding back her tears. Suddenly, she felt something soft brush against the back of her feet. She looked under the bench and there saw Eldora.

The cat hopped up onto the bench and sat down beside Greta. Suddenly, the cat's face morphed and grew long, losing its fur in place of wrinkled skin. Eldora's body likewise grew larger and changed into the elderly Silvana.

Greta was the only one who knew that Silvana had the ability to morph into the cat Eldora. Ever since her time serving beside Victoria as a servant in the Zilonian castle, she and Greta had been close friends.

Greta threw herself into Silvana's arms and started crying. "They've captured the twins and Jack. What if the king reads Jack's mind? We'll all be in trouble. What if Grinage unleashes his dark powers on Kace and Orion?"

Silvana held Greta's hand and gave it a reassuring squeeze. "There's something you need to know about Jack."

Greta stopped crying and looked at the old lady, puzzled.

Silvana kept her gaze steady and continued, "Jack is Bruno's son."

Greta gasped. "That explains the birthmark. How could Bruno have kept such an important secret from me?!"

Silvana's look became stern. "Bruno is alive. He's in the Sheevali Castle."

"Alive? Silvana, have you known this all along? What else are you keeping from me? Was the story about losing Lisa after the escape a lie as well?"

Silvana's features revealed nothing of what she might have been thinking. "Greta, you know I can't tell you everything I learn without putting everyone in danger. There are some secrets that I have to keep until the time is right."

Greta huffed out an exasperated sigh. "Sometimes I wonder which side you're actually on. Tell me the truth about Jack and Lisa, because I'm truly doubting our relationship right now," she demanded.

Silvana shook her head and continued. "We must hope that Bruno will activate Jack's powers before Grinage can read the boy's mind."

"Now I understand why Bruno took that page from Mr. Chapman's book!" Greta exclaimed. "He knew that one day he would find his son and would have to activate the boy's powers. He must have wanted to keep that knowledge from the Sheevali Kingdom. He wanted to keep Jack safe." Greta looked at Silvana with a sudden flash of confusion. "But who is Jack's mother?"

"Her name is Victoria. You must remember her. She was one of Queen Marina's servants and one of my closest friends. She had to stop working at the castle when she was carrying Jack. The day we escaped, I promised Bruno that I would find Victoria and tell her about what happened. I saw her and Jack in the forest that day. We heard the Sheevali king's soldiers behind us. Victoria took my place in the carriage to distract them, giving Lisa, Jack and I a chance to escape. I'm sorry that I didn't tell you about Lisa sooner. I couldn't risk their being exposed, so I kept Jack and Lisa's fate a secret."

Greta eyes grew wide in shock. "What happened then? Where is Victoria now?"

"When the carriage flipped over, Victoria badly hurt her head and lost her memory. Grinage captured her and tried to read her mind, but she wasn't able to remember anything. Ever since then, she has worked in the castle serving Queen Antoinette."

"Did she ever get her memory back?"

Silvana nodded sadly. "Yes, she did, but by then Jack and Lisa were far away, and she didn't know where they were. She wasn't much help for the king."

Greta let out a heavy sigh, the weight of Silvana's information sinking in. "This family has so many secrets. One day, I pray all the secrets will be out in the open and we can discuss our individual histories."

ADMISSION INTO THE ARMY ACADEMY

Jack arrived at the Sheevali castle to be screened for the magic army. He was led through a long, narrow hall and left in a small room with clear glass walls. From his room he could see all of the other cells. Most were filled with boys close to his age, frightened looks on their faces. Some were hugging themselves in the corners of their cells, while other paced like caged animals.

One of the soldiers threw a numbered token at Jack before locking the door. "You're 4 now. When they call you, it's your turn to be tested."

Jack looked around. The place was immaculate and spacious and had stark-white walls running along the outer frame of the building. It was very bright, even though no lamps or lights could be found. It gave Jack a chill, an uneasy feeling running through his veins.

Down the hallway there was a room that emanated a bright-purple light from a strangely shaped, see-through dome in its center. Two men sat behind the dome while a third man ran back and forth between them and the back door.

The boy in the room next to Jack's was called, and he took his place inside the dome. He shook with terror, but he didn't dare ignore the soldiers' instructions.

The light in the dome started blinking and flashing like shooting stars in a galaxy of colorful patterns. The soldiers nodded at the confirmation of the boy's power. One of the men looked at the boy and gave him an order. "Now demonstrate your magic skills to us, boy."

The boy cracked his knuckles with a sharp snap, and the cloth that the men were wearing became covered with metal spikes. The men at the table were satisfied, and the soldiers escorted the boy to the back door.

All of a sudden, Jack saw soldiers bring in two more boys. Despite their appearance, he knew it was Orion and Kace. They were placed in the cell next to his. Their eyes met, but then each looked away quickly, pretending not to know the other.

A voice bellowed down the hall at him. "Number 4, you're up!" It was his turn.

Jack worked to control his fear. He was worried the soldiers would throw him in jail when they found out he had no powers. He'd heard in the tavern that anyone who went into the testing rooms without any powers never came back.

Once out in the middle of the room, Jack was made to stand beneath the dome. At first the lights did nothing. The men whispered among themselves, occasionally looking up with dark glances toward Jack. A door to the back of the room suddenly opened and closed of its own accord. Shortly after, the lights started to blink. One of the men got up and walked around the dome. The lights were still blinking and multiple stars were sparkling.

When the lights stopped blinking a different man came to Jack and gave him a look of suspicion. "It's very strange that the dome didn't detect your power right away. Show us what you have."

Jack squeezed his hands and disappeared. Seconds later he became visible again.

Kace and Orion, watching together from their cell, gasped with surprise. The last time they saw anything of the sort was with Bruno. Kace then looked at his finger and saw that the ring he was wearing had disappeared. He looked at Jack's hand, but his ring was gone as well.

Orion looked at Kace. "Something strange is going on here."

Kace narrowed his eyes. "I think someone is helping Jack."

The back door opened and the soldiers escorted Jack out.

BRIDGET

When Lisa and Alexa walked into the dining hall for breakfast the next morning, everyone was talking about the new girl. Lisa sat down at a table and leaned toward Maya, the girl sitting next to her.

"What's going on?"

Maya looked at Lisa with glee at the chance to do her part in the rumors. "Gabriella left the school yesterday evening because she had some kind of family emergency, and Chantelle got a new roommate. Her name is Bridget. I hear that she has a terrible temper. Ms. Clarantia found Chantelle this morning crying in the bathroom. She doesn't want to talk to anybody about what happened between her and Bridget."

Alexa frowned. "What's Bridget's story?"

Maya shrugged her shoulders. "Nobody knows. The only thing I heard is that she came from a family with eight brothers. She doesn't seem to tolerate anyone who has a different opinion than hers. Some of the girls are saying that she's a daredevil tomboy with a mischievous streak. She doesn't seem to care too much about what others think of her. They also say her family has an herb store and they can create all kind of potions. She's trouble, if you ask me."

Lisa scanned the room. "Where's Chantelle now? I don't see her."

"That's because she was allowed to eat her breakfast in her room with Ms. Gretuala and the new girl. I guess they're trying to figure out if they can stay together and work things out."

As Maya finished her sentence, Chantelle, Bridget, and Ms. Gretuala walked into the room. Everyone suddenly became very quiet.

The two girls sat in the corner and joined the rest of the students eating breakfast. After Lisa and Alexa were done with their food, they stopped by Chantelle and Bridget's table to introduce themselves.

Lisa looked at Chantelle with concern in her eyes. "Are you feeling all right?"

Chantelle nodded sullenly, not looking up to meet Lisa's gaze.

Lisa turned to Bridget and smiled brightly. "My name is Lisa, and this is my friend Alexa. We share a room as well."

Bridget shot the girls a cold look. "You just want to know what happened, right. That's the real reason you came to say hello? Well, we're fine. We just had a small misunderstanding, that's all. I accidentally picked the wrong bed."

Bridget glared at them defiantly.

"I didn't know it was already Chantelle's, and she became very upset with me. Now we're all right. Isn't that true, Chantelle?"

Chantelle nodded and averted her eyes from the girls.

Alexa grabbed Lisa's hand and gave a nervous laugh. "Well if you need anything, we're happy to help you. Chantelle is one of the best and kindest students here. You're very lucky to have her as your roommate."

Bridget handed Chantelle an apple as a sign of trust. "I'm sorry for my behavior. I promise I'll do my best to control my temper. I don't to want to hurt your feelings again."

Lisa and Alexa returned to their table.

"What happened?" Nia and Maya asked at once.

Lisa smiled. "They're going to be fine. Bridget is just adjusting. Chantelle will help her out."

Alexa sent out a powerful thought so that only Lisa could hear. "I'm not so sure, dear sister. Didn't you notice how cold Bridget was? Mark my words, trouble is coming."

THE TWINS ENROLL

It was Kace and Orion's turn to pass the admission test for the army academy. Just before they were taken into the dome, the backdoor opened and another officer walked in. The boys recognized him right away. It was the same man who burned their house down; it was Orlando.

Orlando looked at the twins with a sneering grin. "Hello, again. You got me in a lot of trouble when you escaped under my watch last time. I'll not make that mistake again," he said, gloating over his victims.

Orion looked at him haughtily. "Obviously not big enough trouble, since you're still here."

Kace and Orion could see the veins in Orlando's forehead bulge and the muscles in his jaw grow taut. Orlando shook with anger. But after a moment he steadied his breathing and calmed his temper. He remembered his time spent as a bright-red fly and shivered. The memories still gave him goose bumps. If it hadn't been for Princess Isabella intervening on his behalf, Grinage would've squashed him. Orlando's eye twitched at the memory of the king's hand hovering over him and the princess's sweet voice sounding out from somewhere else in the room to stop it from falling down upon him.

Officer Orlando kept his voice calm. "I see you changed your hair style. We were looking all over for you. Please don't bother to lie to us anymore. Silly parlor tricks won't help you. We know who you are and what your powers are."

Kace and Orion looked at each other and shook their heads back and forth, releasing the magic from their hair and returning to their natural look.

Orlando turned to the other officers. "We can skip the dome test. The king himself wants to see them. Boys, follow me."

Kace and Orion followed reluctantly, but kept their conversation silent.

"How could you come back after I was captured, Orion? Do you even understand what you did?"

"You would have done the same if you were me," answered Orion derisively.

"They didn't have a clue that we were the twins they were looking for. You always have to play the hero and now we're both trapped." Kace shook his head with frustration.

"Orlando would've recognized you anyway. He remembered our faces. He would've tortured you until he found me too. This way we're together and unhurt."

"I guess you might be right. Don't let it go to your head." Kace knew his brother meant well.

Orlando led them through a set of huge metal doors into a spacious room subdivided by arched columns carved in a chevron design. There would have been both a sense of elegance and comfort in the room's design had it not been for the large throne in the middle containing Grinage's distinctive form.

"Hello, Kace. Hello, Orion," Grinage sneered, pretending to be friendly. "I'm glad to see you two are well. I wish we'd had the pleasure of meeting one another many years ago."

"You mean when you tried to kidnap us and destroyed our family?" snapped Kace, his cheeks flushing with outrage.

"I simply underestimated you last time. Now that I see you closely, I notice a bit of my little brother in you. It's so nice to have family."

"We're nothing like you!" Kace barked.

Orion's reached to Kace's shoulder to calm his rage. He knew it would do them no good to go too far.

Grinage chuckled as if Kace's anger was hilarious. "You're a feisty one. You must take after you're father. He always spoke his mind."

"I'm sure he still does," Kace snarled back.

The king came down from his throne and looked closely into the boys' eyes, sending a chill down their spines. "Whether you like it or not, we're family. You are my nephews, and you will help me find your sisters."

Orion, who was standing quietly all this time, looked boldly into the king's eyes. "Our family might have lost the battle, but the war is still to be determined."

A wicked grin spread across Grinage's face. "That's what I like about you boys. You're different from others. The way you handle yourselves and don't give up makes me admire you. It's too bad I'm going to have to break you."

Then Grinage reached his hands toward the boys sending a strong, cold wind wrapping in and around them like tentacles. The boys felt the icy clutch of the king's magic wrap tight inside their chests as he copied their powers with his medallion. Their silent communication, however, was beyond his detection.

When he was finished with them, the boys fell to the floor in a heap. Grinage waved an angry hand at his soldiers. "Take them away to the army academy. I am done with them for now." He then turned and disappeared in a puff of smoke. The soldiers holding the boys began to drag the boys away, they were not going to risk upsetting the king.

FRIENDSHIP

The tailor brought in Bella's birthday dress; it was time to try on his latest creation—each made with the care and dedication of his love for his craft. But this particular gown was a masterpiece. The white lace dress was fitted in the bodice, showing off Bella's feminine shape, and flared out at the waist into a long, flowing skirt. A necklace of large sapphires and diamonds hung around her neck. A translucent white shawl was draped over her shoulder.

"It's done!" The queen whisked into her daughter's quarters with a sing-song melody in her voice. She flopped down onto a chair and let out a breathy sigh. "I spoke with your father. He agreed that it's a terrific idea to have an academy competition for your birthday."

Antoinette looked at her daughter in the mirror and remembered her own days as a young princess. She sighed again and let out a girlish giggle. "When I first met your father, I was swept off my feet by his good looks, his strength, and his boldness. It was in a competition as well. At that time, your father was engaged to a different girl. Her name was Selena, and she was from the Sheevali kingdom. I had a thing with another young man named Arthur. He was your father's biggest competition.

"Your father and Arthur faced off against each other in the competition, and in the middle of their fight, your father caught Arthur looking at me. Your father was sly even then. The second that Arthur was distracted, your father sprang at him! That poor fool Arthur fell to the ground, and I fell for your dad. The intensity in that man and the way he acted instantaneously—I knew I needed a man with that kind of ambition. Afterward, when your father came to gloat over his win, I couldn't help myself. I threw myself into his arms and held him with a deep kiss. That was enough for him to fall for me as well. And because I told them that I was from the Zilonia kingdom and had a royal heritage, your grandfather gave us his blessing."

Antoinette sighed dramatically. "Of course, we were hoping to have a lot of kids together, maybe even a couple of twins, but it didn't work out that way for us. Now your father hopes that you and Antuan will produce twin grandchildren for him."

The queen looked again at her daughter in her elegant gown and grinned. "You're gorgeous, my dear, in any dress, but this one makes you look even more stunning."

Bella stiffened at her mother's compliment, but kept her face placid.

The queen stood up, glanced at herself in the mirror with admiration, and smoothed out her dress. Before she left the room, she paused. "By the way, Bella, have you seen my crystal lamp? It's missing."

Victoria held her breath, and Bella turned to her mother with a guilty look on her face. "I'm so sorry, mother, I meant to tell you... I wanted to see how it would look in my room, and I accidentally broke it."

The queen's cheeks flared red with anger, but she looked at Bella's pained face and calmed her fury. Instead she left the room filled with irritation.

After Antoinette left, Bella turned to Victoria, who was still shivering, and asked, "Something doesn't add up. If my mother is from the Zilonian world and my father is from the Sheevali world, how does that make me only pure Sheevali? Wouldn't I be equally both?"

Victoria got up from her knees and adjusted Bella's shawl. "That's because your mother didn't tell you the entire story."

Bella's eyebrows arched in surprise. "Come, you have to tell me." Bella ran to her bed and motioned for Victoria to sit next to her.

Bella leaned in close, giving Victoria a conspiratorial look. "Tell me all of it."

Victoria held Bella's hand and gave it a squeeze. "You are from the Sheevali world because your mother is from the Sheevali universe also. She wouldn't have had a chance at marrying your father if she didn't choose to lie to King Theodore about having royal roots from the Zilonia kingdom. At that time, King Theodore wanted more than anything to find a royal Zilonian bride for his oldest son, Grinage. Selena was the daughter of the king's closest friend, but she had nothing to do with the Zilonia kingdom. Your father's engagement was made long before the Sheevali king came upon this universe. Once the king found out about the legend of absolute power that would be born from two pairs of twins of parents from two different worlds, he agreed to let his son marry your mother. He believed the lie both of your parents told him. The king and queen were so in love that they would do everything they could to stay together.

"Later when your grandfather found out about the lie, he left this world in anger. I believe they haven't spoken in many years, and now your father has only one daughter. He wants you to marry Antuan because he is one of the Zilonian royals. You marriage could restore his relationship with his father and make him the most powerful king of all time."

"But what about Antuan's mother? Wasn't she a Sheevali spy?" Questions flooded Bella's head. "That would mean Antuan is not purely Zilonian." She thought hard to understand the complicated relationships.

Victoria shook her head. "Jasmine was a very loyal servant to your father, but she was Zilonian born. The word is that she wiled Sebastian with her charms so he'd help her steal the medallion, but instead, she really did fall in love with him. She convinced King Theodore to let them live together under his protection in exchange for the jewel."

"I knew that Antuan lost his mother when he was little but I didn't know how she died," said Bella mesmerized by the story.

"She was killed while trying to flee with the medallion. Sebastian has never gotten over it and till this day blames Zilonia for her death. Antuan is fully Zilonian, and you are fully Sheevali. That's what makes your union so enticing to your father."

As Bella was listening to Victoria, her mouth dropped wide open. "Tell me about the legend of the twins. I want to know everything."

Right at that moment, another servant walked in. "The king is requesting an audience with his daughter."

Bella kissed Victoria on the cheek. "I must go now. We will talk again soon."

Victoria breathed a sigh of relief as Bella departed, but it would only be a matter of time before she found out the whole truth.

BRUNO'S NEWS

Victoria rushed back to her room and flopped down on her bed, breathing hard to catch her breath. A soft knock at her door alerted her. "Who is it?" Victoria's sweet voice chirped from the other side.

"It's me," Bruno whispered.

Victoria opened the door, grabbed Bruno's hand, and dragged him inside.

Bruno had a thrilled look on his face. "I think I just saw our son. Jack is here."

Victoria dropped to the floor, covering her mouth so she wouldn't scream. Her eyes went wide. "Are you sure?"

"Almost positive, but he sure looks like our son. He has the leaf birthmark on his right shoulder, and he looks just like you. I didn't see his eyes, but he has your dark hair. He's very good looking." Bruno winked. "Just like you."

Victoria gasped. "I must see him at once! It took me so long to get better after the amnesia, but since I've had my memory back, I always carry the memory-blocking potion in case the Sheevali king decides to read my mind. I've already had to use it quite a few times now. Every time I take it though I'm afraid that my memory loss will become permanent. Last time it took me a few days to get back to normal."

Bruno's eyebrows knit together with concern. "You should stop taking the potion, Victoria. The king won't find out anything new from you that he didn't already know."

"But what about you? Even though you look different now, I know that it's you. This could be very valuable information for the king. He's never asked me about you before, but with Jack here, what if he does? I'll have to keep my potions close, but I promise not to use them unless it's life or death. Where is Jack? Can I see him?"

Bruno sighed. "He's in a holding room right now. I helped him pass the magical-power test, but he's still in big trouble because he doesn't have his powers yet. If the king reads Jack's mind, who knows what he'll find out. Please wait to see him until I activate his powers. I can't allow Grinage to read his mind. We'll have to be even more careful from now on. Jack is being monitored every minute, but don't worry. I'll find a way to get close to him."

"I hope he remembers us," Victoria whispered, tears rolling down her cheeks. Victoria took the tiny carved figurine of a horse, its rope tail patchy and worn, from her pocket. She always carried it with her, remembering Jack's love for it as an infant. The feeling of the smooth wood beneath her fingertips always helped her regain her memories sooner. The last time she saw Jack, he'd given the toy to her to keep until they met again. She held the figure close to her chest and ached to see him.

"There's one more thing." Bruno said. "Kace and Orion are here too, and Grinage knows who they are. I think it's time to get in touch with Greta."

THE SNEAKY GARDNER

Bridget had always enjoyed her family's beautiful garden; it was relaxing picking the flowers and herbs for the variety of potions made by her family. She'd known happiness, real contentment, drifting through the myriad of flowers at least, until her parents had decided it was time for her to become a lady. Now, these oppressive stone walls and strict class schedule left her homesick.

Bridget was bright but more, she was blessed with an incredible instinct. She always wore a serious expression on her face that reflected itself in the deep, endless fields of her sandy brown eyes. Even her hair looked serious, cascading in sleek honey-hued ribbons long and straight over her shoulders. At home, her brothers always treated her as an equal; they knew that she was no one to mess with—thanks to the time she saved her brother Quinten from a savage dog nearly twice her size.

Thinking back on it, even she shuddered a little. For weeks some beast had been ravaging the surrounding farms, stealing chickens, geese—even a pig. Nothing was left behind but tattered feathers and bones gnawed bare. One day, she and her brothers just happened to be walking along and suddenly this huge dog, snarling and its teeth bared, leaped from the trees and dragged poor Quinten to the ground. Bridget, with no thought for her own safety, came to her brother's aid, throwing her weight against the dog.

Later, her brothers would say that she'd stared the dog down and broke it through sheer force of will. She loved the new sense of respect her brothers gave her. At home she'd felt loved, but at school everything was different, and the only thing that reminded her about her house was the garden.

Bridget walked into the conservatory and saw a gardener hunched over the knotted mound of a thorny rosebush. She plopped down next to him and watched him work for a moment.

"Can I help? I miss working in my family's garden," she asked, her voice soft.

Rufus looked up from his work and smiled at her. "Of course, my dear. Why don't you help me dig some weeds out?" He handed a fresh pair of gloves to her.

Bridget grinned and nodded, moving to her knees and hunching over the base of another bush nearby. "I love flowers too," she sighed. "I enjoy mixing herbs and flowers together to create magical potions."

Rufus beckoned Bridget closer. "I'd love to hear what kind of potions you can make out of roses and other flowers. Please tell me what your favorite elixir is."

Bridget looked fondly at a yellow rose and traced the edges of its velvety petals with her finger. "Yellow roses are the most favorable in my ranch. My favorite potion is 'The Singing Lol'. If you drink it before you go to bed, the next day you'll have the most incredible voice. Everyone will love to hear you sing." Bridget giggled, picturing the effects of the Singing Lol in her mind. "One time, I gave it to my oldest brother, Gregory, and he sang a beautiful love song to his girlfriend Eleanor. Even though Gregory doesn't know how to sing, the potion made his voice sound like an angel. Eleanor still asks him to sing, but he doesn't want to because he wants to keep that moment special and magical."

"You certainly know a lot about your family's trade. I've heard that the Singing Lol is supposed to be a difficult potion to master." Rufus picked up a yellow rose he'd laid on the grass beside him and handed it to Bridget. "I have plenty of roses, and if you want, I'll leave a few of them on this bench for you. They can serve as a reminder of your home."

Bridget smiled with gratitude. She took the rose and ran to the door to put it in water. At the entrance, Bridget stumbled into Lisa and Alexa.

"Hi, Bridget." Lisa gasped as she saw the flower in Bridget's hand. "What a beautiful rose you have!"

Bridget brought the yellow rose to her nose and sniffed its sweet scent. "Rufus gave it to me. He said that I should have it because it would remind me of my home."

Alexa laughed delighted. "We're so glad you're growing comfortable here. It's nice to make new friends."

Bridget turned back to gesture toward the gardener, and Rufus waved at Bridget and the girls. "Come on over, ladies," he called. "I have plenty to go around."

Rufus placed a few red roses into a bucket so the girls could carry them more easily. As he loaded up the bucket, he slipped a tiny insect into one of the flowers that had been charmed to spy on the girls. Bridget saw the tiny, wiggly thing and wanted it more than anything. She stared at it longingly as Lisa and Alexa chattered about how they would display the flowers in their room.

As they walked back to their rooms, Bridget gestured toward the bucket of red roses that Lisa had. "You have a bunch of roses. Can you give me one so I can share with Chantelle? I feel bad about the way I treated her earlier."

To Bridget's delight, Alexa took out the rose with the bug in it and gave it to her. "With pleasure!" Alexa smiled.

Behind them, Bridget could hear Rufus snarling. She turned back curiously, only to find him awkwardly waving at them.

SHARING SECRETS

Victoria was cleaning Queen Antoinette's room when Bella walked in. She looked around furtively before dropping her voice to a whisper. "Are we alone?"

Victoria waived her hand to welcome Bella in. "Yes, your mother is taking a walk with her ladies, Evette and Patricia."

Bella darted to the window and leaned out to make sure her mother was far enough away. "Great! Patricia's hair-do looks exceptionally complicated today. It'll take a while for my mother and Evette to figure out if it's worth instituting as a new trend in the kingdom."

Victoria joined Isabella at the window. "Yes, Ms. Patricia has a very unique form of magic. I wonder what it would be like to wake up every morning with a new hair style."

Both Isabella and Victoria fell into a fit of giggles.

Suddenly, the princess leaned in close to Victoria and in a low voice, said, "Please tell me about the twin legend. After we spoke, I couldn't stop thinking about it."

Victoria looked around the room and nodded. "Fine, but not here. Come with me. I still need to do my chores, and I have to bring more fresh water for the queen."

Together they stepped from the queen's chamber and followed the long hallway that ran along at the same level as the battlements. The wide windows looking out from the hallway provided a sweeping view over the city and of the surrounding area through crafted columns that reached down to marble floors.

Victoria kept her words from carrying. "The legend says that if two royals from two different universes are united together and two sets of twins are born from that union, the twins will have an absolute power. The power can be activated as soon as the youngest twins turn twelve. No one will be able to conquer them."

Bella gasped with anticipation. "Has it ever happened?"

Vitoria nodded sadly. "Just once. Your uncle Christopher, your father's brother, married the Zilonian king's daughter Juliana. Together they had two pairs of twins: two boys and two girls. When the two kingdoms were at war, all of the twins were sent into hiding, and nobody has heard anything from them since."

Bella opened her mouth to ask Victoria another question when she spotted Antuan and his two friends laughing and hollering nearby. One boy, Noah, was a lanky, goofy-looking boy with a blank expression on his face. He had harmless, playful eyes and curly chocolate-colored hair. The other was Francisco. He was much shorter and quite portly with strawberry-blonde hair. Noah was demonstrating his powers by stretching his arms out as far as he could and reaching any object he saw high on the walls: candles, paintings, curtains. Everything he touched oozed with slick slime. As he did so, Francisco would try to jump up and grab the item before Noah could touch it. For his part of the game, Antuan used his powers to freeze the jumping Francisco in midair for a second and prevent him from grabbing the items before Noah slapped them. Bella often saw the boys using this raucous exercise to perfect their timing and precision, and Antuan used it to advanced and show off his abilities. All the boys were quick from years of practice, and their movements appeared to be a blur from Bella's and Victoria's position in the hallway.

Antuan laughed and whooped, taking a moment to turn and wink at Bella as he shot a burst of freezing power at Francisco. But instead of hitting Francisco, Antuan's magic burst pushed Antuan backward against a heavy curtain, bringing it crashing down upon him. Bella watched with amusement as Antuan struggled with the yards of fabric covering him. "I hope you won't be as clumsy as that at the academy competition. The whole kingdom will be laughing."

Antuan gave Bella a sharp look from beneath the heavy woven folds. "Just you wait! I'll be the winner, and you'll be begging me to give you my attention."

Bella laughed, "Keep dreaming! That'll never happen!" She cast a glance at Victoria and mouthed the words, "Thank you." Then she turned and left, deeply drawn to the mystery of the twin children who had been sent into hiding.

FIRED

Rufus lurked in the dark hallway, waiting for Lisa and Alexa to leave their room. All day he was fretting over the failed bug charm. It was his final chance to glean some real information for the Sheevali king; Ms. Clarantia and some of the teachers were watching him suspiciously since he was caught in the conservatory with Lisa and Alexa. Rufus paled at the thought of what Grinage would do to him if he failed in his mission again. The idea of being turned into a fountain stopped his blood cold.

The moment Lisa and Alexa were out the door and away from sight, he rushed into the room. He was in such a hurry that he didn't notice Ms. Clarantia until he bumped into her in the doorway.

"What are you doing in the dormitory?" Ms. Clarantia glared at Rufus with resentment. "You're not allowed anywhere near the girls' rooms.

Rufus stammered and wrung his hands together, trying to find an explanation he wasn't ready to give. "I, umm...I gave Lisa and, ah, Alexa some flowers, but now I need them back because I ran out of red roses. Without them," he stuttered, "my arrangement will be incomplete. Heh..."

Ms. Clarantia looked at him with disbelief and outrage, a little vein bulging at her neck. She stepped toward him and, despite her short stature, made as if to loom over him. Rufus stepped back from her, but she followed with her face nearly pressed to his until his back hit the opposite wall. He slid down low and cowered from her.

"I've seen you lurking around those girls before, asking them too many questions and now sneaking into their room. Why are you so interested in them? This is highly inappropriate."

"I was just being friendly..." The words fell flat even as they left his mouth.

She pointed an angry finger toward the exit to the girls' dormitory. "I do not want to hear your lame excuses. Leave now. I never want to see you in this area again, and I will personally certify that you never approach those girls."

Rufus bowed in humiliation and slunk away. I've really screwed up this time. It's only a matter of time before they toss me out now. Looks like it's time for the contingency plan, he chided himself.

He slunk down the hall away from the dormitories, angry at himself for getting caught. He was so upset that he almost didn't notice the prickly feeling on the back of his neck alerting him to someone following him. He took a sharp turn down a narrow hallway and stopped to wait. When no one appeared, he continued on his way.

Retreating to the garden, Rufus set about making two poisons as a final attempt. He went to the far corner of the conservatory where he dug up two knobbed and gnarled roots that oozed a strange slime. He held one up to his nose and sniffed deeply. A sinister grin spread across his face.

"Ah, the fresh smell of dung this root has is like perfume to my nose."

He took some of the ooze and dropped it onto his poison nail, muttering an incantation under his breath. A foul poison poured from the nail into two small vials, filling them to the top.

After the mixing was complete, he stashed them in a secret place under the mosaic floor next to the entrance. All along he'd had a backup plan in place in case he was discovered, though he had to use it sooner than he'd anticipated. Now it would be up to the other spy to put his poisons to good use.

Just as Rufus stood up from the mosaic on the floor, Ms. Clarantia came storming into the garden, waving a signed paper. "And what are you up to now? Have you been pulling tiles out of our fine art?"

Rufus shook with fear. "I simply dropped my handkerchief." He held a dirty cloth out to her. She jumped away from the smudged and stained cotton square.

"Don't spread your horrible germs here. Put that away!" She thrust the paper into Rufus's hand and gestured toward the front gate. "Ms. Gretuala and I agree that you pose a danger to our students. You will leave immediately and never return."

Rufus let out a sigh of relief that he'd been able to distract her from his hiding space. He gave her a low bow. "As you wish, my lady." You'll get everything you deserve, he thought.

THE SPARK

Bella looked out from her window into the field and sighed. Despite the morning being warm and the birds chirping and flitting about the blooming trees and garden, there was a chill in her heart. Down below, preparations were underway for the student competition her mother had suggested.

Antoinette spared no expense for Bella's special day. The lawn was neatly trimmed and lined with walkways. At the far end of the field were tiered benches set up for the audience, and closest to the castle was the royal pavilion. Bella could picture her father's and mother's thrones set up in all their glory, with fine silks and pillows for ultimate comfort. For Bella's throne, Grinage had made a gesture both cruel and sweet; it was carved to resemble a crown and decorated with the stones he'd collected from his fountains.

As she watched the servants scurrying about the lawn, Bella could see that the preparations were nearly complete. Already cadets were milling about and audience members taking their seats.

Victoria entered the room behind Bella and let out a disappointed tut. "Dear, you're not ready? You know your father and your mother are expecting to see you shortly. Where are your servants?"

Isabella allowed herself another sigh. "I told them not to bother coming in early this morning. I just wanted to get a bit more sleep." And put off this engagement as long as possible, she thought.

Victoria gave Bella a knowing smile. "Come, dear. Let's get you ready." Victoria helped Bella into her dress and piled Bella's hair atop her head in an intricate style. When she was finished, Victoria nodded in satisfaction. "It's time. Everyone is waiting for you."

When Bella walked out to the field, she paused a moment and looked at all of the young soldiers who were cheering for her. Everyone gasped at her beauty and commanding presence. She walked with her head held high like a true royal, allowing a slight smile to play upon her lips, but inside she was roiling with dread and excitement. Her white-lace birthday gown heightened her sophisticated look, and many of the boys were openly gawking at her. She twisted the stem of the flower she held nervously as she made her way to the pavilion.

She spotted Antuan standing at the steps to the podium where the thrones were set and winced as he met her eye. Her flower fell to the ground.

Jack was standing right at the entryway, last in line, when he saw Isabella. Her beauty mesmerized him, and he watched her with deep interest. When he saw her stop in her path and drop her flower, he knew something must have startled her. Following her gaze, Jack saw that Isabella was looking at Antuan, but it was her sudden rigidity that told Jack she hated the boy who stood waiting for her.

Without thinking, Jack darted forward and scooped the flower up off the ground. He held it out for Isabella to take and gave her his most charming smile. "I believe you dropped this." Jack bowed his head and dropped his voice to a whisper. "Don't give him power over you by letting him see you nervous. Let him sweat for your attention."

Bella's mouth dropped open at Jack's boldness, and her face turned a bright red. Behind her, her ladies tittered and giggled, peering at Jack over Bella's shoulder. Bella gulped and took the flower from Jack's outstretched hand. "Thank you for the flower and your courage. I really needed that."

With her head held high, Bella strutted down the aisle toward the pavilion with her ladies crowded like hens behind her. Jack watched her as she walked, completely drawn into her newfound confidence. He let a smirk play across his face as he watched her stride right past Antuan without even acknowledging the boy's presence.

But Jack openly laughed when he saw the look of rage that clouded Antuan's handsome visage upon being ignored. At that moment, Antuan looked at Jack and his face spasmed into an angry snarl. For a moment, their eyes locked and narrowed in mutual contempt.

Kace put a hand on Jack's shoulder and Jack turned around, unlocking his gaze from Antuan's. Kace had a look of concern on his face. "How can you be so foolish? You're making more enemies when we already have an entire kingdom against us. We need to stay out of sight, not flaunt ourselves in front of the royal family."

But Jack wasn't listening; at that very moment Bella had looked his way and gave him the barest hint of a smile. His stomach flipped as their eyes met, and he realized that there was a connection of sorts between them. Kace was right, this did spell trouble but he wasn't sure he could stop.

UNCLE

The cadets all stood in a tight circle in the middle of the field, chatting and laughing until the competition was ready to begin. Two soldiers approached the group and motioned for the cluster of trainees to split down the middle; each half was sent to a different side of the field as horns were sounded.

In the confusion, Jack was separated from Kace and Orion and herded to the other side of the field. Kace still seethed at Jack for picking a fight with Antuan.

"Augh! Can you believe that guy?"

"Looks like you two made a friend." Kace and Orion tensed at the third voice.

"Who—?" Kace jumped. The boys turned to see a man in a black hood. "Hi, boys. I'm happy to see you." The man standing behind them pulled back his hood discretely just enough for the boys to see his face.

Both boys gasped in unison. "Bruno?!"

"Don't be so obvious! You'll give me away in a heartbeat. Just keep facing forward and act like the competition is the most interesting thing you've ever seen."

Kace and Orion did as Bruno said, but beneath their silence they were a flurry of excitement. "Uncle Bruno, you're alive! We thought we'd lost you forever!" Orion exclaimed.

"Yes, I survived, but I can't explain everything now. We don't have much time. For now, tell me, how do you know that boy Jack?"

Kace looked across the field toward Jack. "He came from a different world with Lisa. He's her brother and he saved Alexa when our house was compromised."

Despite himself, Bruno let out an audible gasp. "Lisa is here? Did you find your aunt Greta?"

"Yes," said Orion, "And the girls are staying at the Fairyton Institute right now under her protection. Jack is a great guy, and he really cares about his sister. We're just worried that if the king reads Jack's mind he'll reveal our plan to save our parents."

Kace piped in. "Greta gave Jack a potion that will block his memory. We were lucky that it wasn't confiscated during the admission."

Orion's eyes went wide, and he swung back to look at Bruno. "Uncle Bruno, was it you who helped Jack in admissions?" Suddenly Orion remembered himself and turned back to face the field, hoping he'd gone unnoticed.

"Yes." Bruno answered. "I saw the way you were looking at him, and I realized that he was important to you. I also saw the birthmark on his shoulder. I need to confirm that he is who I think he is."

There was a pause before Kace asked, "What do you mean by that?"

"That's a long story. Right now I need to figure out a way to get you out of here."

Orion gestured toward the pavilion where Grinage sat on his throne. "We also have to retrieve the medallion from the king. Greta told us about how it was stolen from our kingdom, and as long as the Sheevali king possesses it, we will always be in danger."

Bruno's voice was rich with pride as he spoke silently to his nephews. "You've both done remarkably well without me. Don't fear about the medallion. I will find out where the king keeps it at night. Then we will coordinate a plan to take it and get you boys out of here at the same time. We won't have much time, because if Grinage catches us we'll never get another chance to fulfill your destiny."

SAVING NIA

As Fiona and Beatrice were passing by the twins' room, they heard a thump. The girls looked at each other in surprise then darted for the door. Inside, Nia was collapsed on the floor. Her skin had a gray pallor and a thin sheen of sweat dotted her forehead. Beatrice rushed to her side screaming.

"Nia! Wake up! What's wrong?" Beatrice shook Nia hard, but the fragile-looking girl didn't respond. Nia had a rose clutched in her hand, and Beatrice went to move it, but Fiona slapped Beatrice's hand away.

"Don't touch it. It looks like it was poisoned. Go and run for help!"

Beatrice ran out of the room screaming. "Help! Please, somebody! We need help!"

Lisa and Alexa heard Beatrice's cries as they were returning from a visit with Salvador. As soon as her screams reached their ears, the twins went into a frantic sprint. Darting into the room, Lisa and Alexa found Fiona hunched over Nia's prone figure. Fiona cried and shook, wailing over Nia's limp body.

"No!" Lisa screamed and rushed to Nia's side. Lisa took Nia's hand in her own and concentrated hard on healing her friend. "Please, please come back!" But Nia didn't move.

Alexa was locking the door when Lisa looked up at her with desperate tears. "She's not getting better. I can't do this. I need your help."

Alexa rushed to Lisa's side and placed her hands gently over Lisa's, willing her own power into her sister with a gentle squeeze of her fingers.

Fiona let out a gasp as warm light surrounded the girls. The light grew brighter until it was almost blinding. Suddenly the light winked out, and Fiona opened her eyes to see Lisa and Alexa hovering over a weak but living Nia.

Banging on the door and the cries of Ms. Gretuala and Ms. Clarantia brought Fiona out of her stupor. She stood shakily and opened the door. Seeing Nia on the floor, Ms. Clarantia gave a sharp look to Fiona. "What happened?!" But Fiona stood dumbstruck. She'd never seen anything like this.

Fiona's voice was almost a whisper and her eyes wide and wild. "It was unbelievable."

Beatrice pointed to a yellow and a red rose that lay on the floor. "Don't touch those roses. We think they're poisoned."

Nia held her hand up to her face, seeing that her fingers were red and swollen where she had touched the flowers.

"I wanted to put the flowers into the vases so they wouldn't wilt. The moment I touched the yellow rose, the thorn stung me and I fainted."

Other students, drawn by Beatrice's screams, began filing into the room. Chantelle poked her head in and immediately recognized the roses. "Those look like the roses from my room, but mine are missing. I was wondering where they were! Bridget told me that since Rufus was gone, she wanted to add some kind of potion to them to make them last longer."

Ms. Gretuala turned to the cluster of students and called out. "Has anybody seen Bridget?" Each student shook her head no.

Lisa's gaze darted to Alexa. "If Rufus is no longer here, that leaves only Bridget."

Ms. Gretuala leaned and whispered something into Ms. Claratina's ear. Ms. Claratina turned to Fiona and Beatrice. "Come with me, girls. No questions." She turned and stormed out of the room.

Ms. Gretuala raised her hands above the crowd of students to command their attention. "Everyone, go back to your rooms. There's nothing more to see here."

As the students cleared out, Ms. Gretuala helped Nia to her bed for some rest. She issued silent instructions to her nieces to stay safe and to stay in their rooms before she rushed to her office. The silent threat hanging over the school for all these years had become something tangible and dangerous. The attack she had long dreaded had come.

TRUST

The air was thick with tension and Fiona found herself pacing back and forth. She was in the office with Beatrice and her mother as they waited for Ms. Gretuala.

"Something doesn't make sense here. Mother, what did Ms. Gretuala whisper in your ear that made you so nervous? Why did you rush us here? Are we in trouble?"

Ms. Clarantia didn't make a move, just barked, "I don't know what's going on, but I've never seen the principal so cold and focused. It frightens me to think of what might leave her that way. Be patient and sit here. We'll find out what's happening soon enough."

The moment Fiona's backside hit the bench beside Beatrice, the principal walked in and sat down at her desk. Greta gave the girls a hard look and began straightening the papers splayed out in front of her. "I need you to tell me exactly what you saw."

Fiona and Beatrice passed a look between themselves before Fiona opened her mouth to speak. Her voice sounded tight and complexion pale. "We were on our way to a tutorial class when we heard a noise like something falling, so we went into the room. Nia was there unconscious. I...I thought she was dead. I told Beatrice to run for help while I stayed behind with Nia." Fiona's eyes grew wide as she spoke. "That's when Lisa and Alexa came back. Lisa held Nia's hands, but nothing happened. Then Alexa joined her and there was suddenly this bright light—brighter than anything; that's when Nia woke up."

Greta slammed the papers she had gathered on the desk, causing everyone to jump. Beatrice let out a little squeak. When Greta spoke again, her voice had a terrifying calm to it. "Have you spoken to anyone about this?" She looked Fiona straight in the eyes.

Fiona shook her head vigorously. "I haven't. I swear."

"I've been with them the whole time," Ms. Clarantia cut in. "No one has approached them since the incident happened."

Fiona looked down at her shoes and burst out. "We think that Lisa and Alexa are hiding something. They share a special connection, not just friendship. It's like they're related or something." Before Fiona finished her sentence Ms. Gretuala held her hand up, interrupting her.

Ms. Gretuala's voice was firm. "You do not tell this to anybody. Keep it a secret or we will all pay for your indiscretion. If the Sheevali king finds out about this, he will destroy the entire school and we will all be his prisoners."

The girls shook with fear. "We promise," they said at once without daring to ask any questions.

Greta let out her breath in a long sigh that made her look ten years older and gave the girls a warm glance. "Thank you, girls. You may go back to your rooms now and get some rest. Just remember what I've told you."

Fiona and Beatrice padded out of the room with their shoulders hunched and weary, but Ms. Clarantia stayed behind. She came to Greta who was staring numbly at the picture of her family she had taken from a drawer. "Who are those girls? I couldn't help noticing that you're protecting them."

Greta exhaled deeply, continuing to stare at the picture. "Lisa and Alexa have a very rare power that can't get into the Sheevali king's hands." Her eyes darted to Ms. Clarantia in a furtive gesture.

"What sort of power is it? And what kind of danger are we talking about?" Ms. Clarantia's eyes grew wide with fright.

Greta shook her head sadly and averted her eyes from her old friend. "I'm so sorry. That is all I can tell you now, but I promise that when the time is right I will tell you the entire story. I trust you, but the less you know right now, the safer you and the girls will be. I can block King Grinage from my mind, but you cannot. The less you know, the safer we all are."

Ms. Clarantia patted Greta's hand for reassurance. "We've known each other for a long time, and I've never seen you like this before. But I know one thing: you would never let any of us in the school be in danger without a reason. You sacrificed so much, and if you are hiding something it means that it has to be that way."

Greta smiled weakly at Ms. Clarantia's words and placed a hand on her friend's. "My friend, can I count on you?"

Ms. Clarantia looked into Greta's eyes with resolve and said, "Yes. You can. I'll talk to Fiona and Beatrice and make sure that they won't tell a soul about Lisa and Alexa. And if you need my help with anything, just let me know." She then gave her friend's hand a squeeze and took her leave.

COMPETITION BEGINS

The excitement in the air was palpable just before the competition was ready to begin. As part of the opening ceremony, each student received a bow and arrow. Sebastian strode out into the middle of the field with a confident swagger, the audience's cheer a deafening roar.

"Cadets, you have the honor to serve the most powerful of kings." Sebastian turned to Grinage and bowed elegantly. "To open up these proceedings, I will now demonstrate to one and all just what a real soldier of the Sheevali Kingdom should be capable of."

At his signal, the cadets aimed their bows and arrows at him. Sebastian revealed a long strip of fabric, presenting it to the spectators, and he tied the fabric over his eyes as a blindfold. Reaching down, he picked up the bucket of freshly picked flowers.

Sebastian held the flowers high over his head for all to see, and then sent a surge of magic up into the stems, transforming them into shining golden spheres that rotated around his hands at blurred speed. The horn blared out again, and the chosen students aimed and then fired their arrows directly at Sebastian. With the sound from the audience rising to a crescendo, Sebastian, his eyes blindfolded and using only the golden spheres, deflected every arrow that came his way, each falling harmlessly to the ground. His power was supreme and envied by all.

Kace's and Orion's eyes grew wide at the spectacle playing out in front of them.

"Holy cow, is this what we're up against?" Kace gasped.

Orion didn't answer, but the look of defeat on his face said it all.

It was truly spectacular. Even Grinage seemed impressed, slapping his thigh with excitement each time an arrow met one of the orbs and tumbled away.

As Sebastian's performance came to a close and he made his triumphant bow, the general had the honor of announcing the names of the students in each competition pairing. He spun the wheel that listed all of the students' names with great gusto.

"Noah is the first contender. Let's see who his opponent will be!" The crowd cheered and the wheel was spun again. They watched the rotations gradually slowing and the second name selected was Francisco.

"A fair rival for Noah," cried Sebastian, motioning to the cadets to step forward. The spectators went wild with excitement.

The boys left their places and stood before the royal pavilion, the field darkening around them as a thick fog curled upwards from the green lawn. When the fog receded and the light of day returned, a huge swamp appeared where the field once was.

The general called out to the crowd. "The first cadet to reach the other side will be the winner!"

The competitors gamely shook hands and looked into each other's eyes.

"Don't expect me to show you any mercy, my friend," Noah warned.

"Likewise...loser," Francisco scoffed.

The horn bleated to signal the start of the competition. At its first note, the boys ran as fast as they could toward the swamp. Bugs hovered thick in the air over the stagnant water; there were lazy bubbles popping at its surface and releasing a putrid stench. In the center of the swamp, hovering high above the water and too numerous to count, were sparkling golden shapes—triangles, squares, hoops, and others strangely curved or with sharp points. Here and there, like tiny islands, were clumps of damp soil and slimy tangles.

Noah was immediately the faster of the two. He leapt onto the first island, landing heavily. As he did so, the soil beneath his feet began to crumble, falling away into the water. And down with it he sank.

Francisco saw Noah struggling and leapt as far as he could using his powers to increase his stretch, aiming for a spot further off. He landed solidly and without sinking.

"Are you comfortable there?" Francisco laughed. "Your slimy powers are not going to help you beat me."

Noah saw his chance and aimed both of his hands at Francisco, stretching them as far as he could across the swamp. The audience gasped and shrieked.

"Get back where you belong, you jumping frog," snarled Noah.

With his hands fully extended, Noah grabbed Francisco by the shoulders and whipped him backwards and off balance, pulling him onto the same tiny island. One against the other, they struggled to hold their ground. As they did so, a golden ring passed within reach. Francisco jumped and made a grab for it, hoping to use it as a weapon against Noah. Instead, the ring carried him away toward the other side of the swamp.

"See you on the other side, slime face," shouted Francisco, grinning from ear to ear.

Noah watched Francisco approaching the other side, hands tight to the strange golden circle. With a growl, he leaped up and latched onto one of his own while at the same time readying a ball of slime.

"I am not done with you yet," yelled Noah.

Holding on with one hand and aiming with the other, Noah threw the slime directly at Francisco's hand. It landed squarely.

Francisco let loose his grip and plunged head first into the swamp.

His foe vanquished and a smile on his face, Noah, his elongated arms reaching out ahead of him, caught one shining object after another, and with a smooth easy rhythm, swung across to the other side before Francisco had the chance to pull himself gasping from the foul-smelling muck. As he jumped onto the winner's platform, his arms raised in victory, the crowd burst into applause.

SMALL VICTORY

With everyone's eyes on the competition, Jack saw his chance. He sneaked around the edge of the field and rejoined Kace and Orion.

Approaching them, Jack brought his voice down to a whisper. "How am I supposed to participate in this competition? They're going to figure out that I don't have any powers."

Kace and Orion shook their heads in unison. Kace frowned in concentration. "We can't exactly fake a power. But maybe we can distract everyone to keep them from noticing."

Orion brightened. "What if I make the spinning wheel so tiny that they can't read it?"

"It's nice of you to volunteer your powers," Jack sighed. "But if you help me like that, the Sheevali king will realize we're all in this together."

"Jack's right," said Kace. "The only advantage we have right now is that nobody suspects that Jack is with us. We need something that won't connect him to us."

"Let's hope that Bruno will help us if Jack's name gets picked like he did last time," said Orion scanning the area looking for the black hood in the crowed.

Jacks eyes bulged. "Your uncle is here? I thought it was strange that I passed the admission test that easy."

At that moment, General Sebastian called out Kace's name. All three boys turned toward the pavilion to see Grinage whispering something into the general's ear. Sebastian left the king's side and returned to his place on the podium. "This next competition will be between newcomers Kace and Orion!"

"Figures," Kace whispered to Orion.

The boys stepped forward onto the field. They kept their gaze straight ahead, but Kace continued to speak just low enough to keep anyone else from hearing. "I want you to have the honor of winning this competition. This game is just a distraction."

Orion rolled his eyes. "I don't care about Grinage's silly games. If you want you can have this show-off victory."

"No," Kace replied. "You came back for me, and I want everyone to think that you're the strongest. We both know that you're usually the brain. I appreciate you letting me be the muscle."

Orion laughed. "Muscle-brained is more like it! But I'm very proud to be your brother."

As the twins made their way out onto the field, the general raised his hands in a flourish. "The last field was a little murky. What do you say we heat things up? Boys, are you ready for 'Passing the Fire'?"

The audience erupted into a roar as Grinage sent out a surge of magic and they watched it swirl around the field. The air grew dark as the magic created a vortex of energy, summoning a deep mist. When everything cleared, Kace and Orion found themselves standing at the edge of a steep ravine. Down below, lava flowed slow and hot, while greedy flames licked upwards toward their feet.

Kace looked down to the bottom of the ravine. "I don't think this is real. It's got to be an illusion, right?"

Orion tore a strip of cloth from his sleeve and let it drop down toward the bottom. The fabric burst into flames, burning away before it even reached the lava. "It looks pretty real to me."

Kace patted his brother on the back. "Let's just get across quickly; this is just a test of our powers."

Orion shrugged. "If we refuse to play along he'll just send us to jail. We might as well give him what he wants."

"Well then, here goes nothing." As the horn sounded, Kace's eyes darted toward a bench filled with instructors. Kace grinned at the instructors and said under his breath, "Time to stretch your legs." He raised his hand and pointed at the bench signaling to Orion to join in, who did so. With a flourish of his hands, he shrunk it down to a tiny size, leaving the teachers sprawling on the ground.

The spectators and cadets erupted with laughter while Kace brought the bench high over the pit. As he did so, Orion widened and elongated it so that it spanned the length of the field. "High five to us," Orion laughed, encouraged by the enthusiasm of the crowd.

Once the bench was large enough, Kace brought it down with a heavy slam that sent up a cloud of dust, obscuring the entire field. In the confusion, Kace and Orion darted across their new bridge to the other side. By the time the dust had cleared, both boys were standing together on the other side of the field, their arms raised high in victory.

For a moment the twins locked eyes with Grinage who stared at them with some malice. Orion muttered under his breath. "I don't think that the king realizes that this is just the start of what is to come."

"Maybe not," Kace breathed heavily. "But there's much to do before we can claim victory and power is restored to our family."

FORGIVENESS

A tentative knock roused Alexa, Lisa, and Nia from their seats on Nia's bed.

"Come on in!" Nia called out, her voice still weak.

After a moment, the door opened slowly and Beatrice and Fiona peered into the room. They stood silently looking at Nia, both wearing looks of guilt and shame. Nia returned their silence with a sweet smile and patted a space on the bed.

"You asked us to come?" Fiona fidgeted nervously.

"I wanted to say thank you for helping me. If you hadn't arrived when you did, I'm afraid the worst could have happened."

Fiona looked stricken. "We're very sorry for being mean to you before. Our behavior was, well, it was unacceptable. Please forgive us?"

Beatrice added, "We were so competitive that we completely forgot about winning the right way. It was stupid...and selfish." Her gaze darted to Lisa and Alexa. "Please don't worry about either of us letting information about you out. Your secret is safe with us. Nobody needs to know that you have these unbelievable powers."

Nia shared a look between Lisa and Alexa before turning back to Fiona and Beatrice with the same wide grin. "I knew you two weren't as mean as you've been acting. I always thought that you must have some goodness in you. Here you both are proving me right. Of course I accept your apology."

"Friends!" Alexa said delightedly, sending the other girls into laughter.

When Fiona and Beatrice were leaving, Alexa and Lisa looked at Nia as if to ask her a question. Before they could say anything, Nia nodded. "I think you're right. This feud is over."

"No more cheating for us," Beatrice smiled.

Lisa called out to Fiona and Beatrice. "Wait. We'll go with you. We want to give you the video."

Fiona and Beatrice spun back around and looked at Lisa with delight. Fiona looked like she would almost leap for joy. "You'll really let us have it? We didn't think we deserved to get it after the way we acted."

"There's no point harboring a grudge. It's all in the past now." Lisa smiled at them. "Come on."

Together, the five girls ventured out into the hallway and then to the room where the scoreboard was kept. Lisa pointed toward the curtain where she'd hidden from Beatrice. "There. It's behind the curtain and beneath the loose floorboard."

Fiona laughed out loud. "That hiding spot is brilliant! I would never have thought to look there. We thought it was in your room this entire time."

The girls all looked at each other and laughed. Alexa bent down behind the curtain, pulling the floorboard up, and retrieved the memory card. Suddenly, she heard a rustling sound coming from within the wall. "Quiet, everyone! Did you just hear that?"

The girls looked at each other wide eyed and all nodded in agreement.

"Somebody's behind the wall," Beatrice whispered. "Maybe it's Bridget hiding from the principal. Everybody is still looking for her."

Fiona and Beatrice rushed to the wall and started pounding on it with their fists. "Come out, Bridget! We know you're there!" But the only answer they received was the sound of departing footsteps.

RIVALRY

The king himself decided to announce the last two rivals. It hadn't passed unnoticed that Antuan appeared unsettled when the new boy picked up the flower, and he thought it would be entertaining to prod Antuan further. He rose from his throne and basked in the cheers of the audience. Having had his fill, he raised his hand and everyone grew suddenly silent. "For our final competition, I have decided to choose the rivals myself." He extended his hand out to Antuan. "Antuan, step forward." Then he pointed at Jack. "Your name?"

Jack looked about to be certain that the king was addressing him before he looked back at Grinage and gulped. "Jack," he answered tensely but with clarity, masking the edge of fear he felt inside.

"Come and join us," the king summoned.

Jack and Antuan stood together at the edge of the field and faced the crowd. Grinage continued. "I am told that Jack has the ability to make himself invisible, and while that's impressive, it will not be very entertaining. So instead of a match between powers, this will be a match of wits and speed. Powers are forbidden for this round!" The crowd cheered with excitement, but Grinage had more to say. "And since there is no magic, these boys will have much to endure. The cadet who completes this challenge will be declared the winner. I will not leave you disappointed today though. You came to see these boys' incredible powers, so I will make sure you get what you came for." The crowd cheered and Grinage continued, "You already know about Antuan's impressive skills, which one day will grow into one of the most remarkable abilities our kingdom has ever seen. Being able to detect an enemy's power is a dream for every soldier, but when it comes with the combination of being able to freeze them on the spot, it makes this gift even more extraordinary. Few of you have seen Jack's power; so before the competition begins Jack will demonstrate his ability before you all."

Grinage gestured toward the sky. "The winner of this round will be the first to send their message above the field by catching a magic bubble and throwing it up as high as they can. Two gloves are placed within the field, and one cadet will have to collect both gloves to complete this task as the orbs are very dangerous. Once the bubble is thrown into the air, we will all see it explode into a prophecy of the winner's future! We will begin once Jack displays his power. Let the best soldier win!"

Antuan exuberantly waved at the crowds and snarled at his opponent. "Are you ready to be humiliated, Jackie boy?

Jack ignored the remark. He was too concerned about having to show his powers, or rather, the lack of them.

Jack glanced behind him at Isabella, hoping that her face would give him courage. She caught him looking at her and gave a barely perceptible nod of reassurance. He let out a deep breath as he looked into her eyes. He could see a glimmer of hope reflected in them, and it made him feel strong.

Jack closed his eyes, squeezed his hands as he had done in the dome, and vanished from sight. A moment passed, and he appeared again where he'd been standing before. The entire audience let out a cheer, but Kace and Orion were cheering loudest of all. They'd seen Bruno's hooded figure appear near the edge of the field and leave just as quickly once Jack reappeared.

Kace slapped Orion on the shoulder in his excitement. "Did you see him?"

"Yes, Bruno is our man!" Orion beamed. "Now let's watch Jack and Antuan compete. This should be interesting!"

Again the lights dimmed low and the field was masked in a deep fog. When the light returned, a stretch of dark mud appeared. Right behind the muddy field, there was a lake rimmed with thick foam. On the side closest to Jack and Antuan, but beyond the field of mud, was a tall pole with a special glove at the top. A rope bridge spanned the length of the lake leading to a second pole with another glove. Small electric orbs zipped about at the far end of the field beyond the lake and near the royal family, ready to be caught.

Jack eyed the lake and the foam surrounding it. What's making all of that foam? He wondered. He quickly stopped guessing because his eyes once again met with Isabella, who was sitting quietly watching the competition. He wanted with all of his might to impress the princess, but he knew that Antuan couldn't afford to lose the competition in front of the entire academy and his father.

"I almost feel sorry for you, newcomer, but you'll have to learn your place." Antuan taunted, jutting out his chin defiantly.

"Buckle up your seat belt. You're about to experience the rollercoaster of defeat, snooty boy," replied Jack.

Antuan looked confused. "What are you talking about?"

Jack smirked at Antuan and got into a ready position.

At the sound of horn, both boys ran toward the pole with the first glove, both falling into the thick, sticky mud at the same time. The mud clung to them, slowing their steps as they waded forward. The boys struggled against the thickness of the sludge at their feet and against each other, pushing and shoving as they scrambled across the field.

Aggravated by the boldness of his challenger, Antuan exclaimed, "Get out of my way, you simpleton. Go back to the rat hole that you came from."

Jack was amused. "I'm just warming up. This is going to be a bumpy ride for you." It gave him a sense of pleasure knowing that his rival was confused by his slang.

Antuan tried to push Jack down into the sludge, saying in his most arrogant tone, "I don't know why you bother, flower boy. You have no chance against me."

Jack ignored the flower remark and pushed Antuan back, his legs churning hard against the mud. "Is that here in the field or there with Isabella?"

Infuriated by Jack's daring and insolence, Antuan changed direction and threw all of his weight against the unsuspecting Jack, knocking the boy off balance, his head disappearing below the surface.

"Ha, who's on top now?" Antuan crowed triumphantly as he yanked himself out of the mud and onto the first pole. Up he went rather effortlessly and grabbed the glove. Jack's head broke the surface just in time to see Antuan spiraling down with the first glove and said, "You won't get the second one without a fight!"

The first pole lost, Jack changed direction and made for the second one, which meant getting up to the rope bridge. Fortunate for him, his arms were just long enough to take hold of the lower strand and pull himself up. Though the weight of the mud on his shoes was more than he had expected, he still managed to swing his feet out of the sludge and up to the rope, crossing his ankles to gain hold. Seconds later he was up on the bridge and moving toward his goal. Feeling good about himself, he looked back to where Antuan was and shouted, "There's a great view of the pavilion from here, royal thrones and all."

Moving as fast as he could, he was about halfway when he felt an unsettling bounce at his feet and the bridge itself grow slack. Jack looked back at Antuan, who had produced a silver knife from the waist of his pants.

The smug suitor had an impish grin on his face. "Time for a bath!" he yelled and brought the blade down with a sharp thunk.

The rope unspun its strands and snapped. Jack hit the water hard, the current spinning him about and pulling him under. He sputtered to the surface, disoriented and gasping for breath. His ears popping, he heard a splash behind him; Antuan was headed his way. I've got to get out of here! The words screamed in his head while his powerful arms pulled through the water like oars.

Jack began swimming toward the other end of the lake but soon realized that he wasn't making any progress. Instead, he was slowly being pulled farther from the shore. The foam that lined the lake had disguised the strong current within the water. He tried to let the force of the current carry him toward the ropes that were now dangling in the water, but to no avail.

Looking back, he saw Antuan swimming powerfully across the current, his brawny form gliding easily toward the other side, the current propelling him forward. Jack followed, and in moments both boys were out of the water with the second pole right in front of them.

When Jack reached the pole, Antuan was already on his way up.

"You sneaky little slime," hollered Jack. "You really have no honor."

"We call it being resourceful," Antuan shouted back, looking down at Jack with a condescending grin.

Jack looked around frantically for a way to beat Antuan to the prize. He spotted a length of rope from the bridge. As quickly as he could, Jack tied a knot in the rope and coiled it around his elbow. He swung the end around fast, launching the length of rope at the glove like a slingshot. Just as Antuan reached for the glove, Jack's rope hit it sending it down to the ground at his feet.

Looking up at the surprised Antuan, he smirked. "Now that's what you call being resourceful."

As the infuriated Antuan slid down the pole and came barreling toward him, Jack slipped on the glove, just in time to avoid Antuan's heavy fist as it hurtled toward his face.

"You are not stealing my victory, newcomer." Every vein on Antuan's face popped out in anger.

Jack was quick, dodging the attack with ease. He swung back, landing a glancing blow to Antuan's chin.

"Who is smiling now?"

Antuan staggered backward but righted himself quickly, lunging at Jack. Together they entangled and fell to the ground in a flurry of dust and wild swings.

Grunting and breathing hard as he sought to drive his elbows into Jack's ribs, Antuan said, "I like your spirit, new boy. But I'm top dog around these parts."

Fending off most of the blows with his forearms, Jack managed to hook the bigger boy's leg with his own and throw him off, both boys simultaneously getting to their knees. "You might be the top dog around here," he said between deep breaths, "but you're about as threatening as a puppy."

Antuan was the first to his feet, and as Jack rose to face off against him, he slipped a tiny capsule from his pocket into his hand.

"Here, let's shake hands."

Before Jack was fully prepared, Antuan lunged at him. But Instead of taking Jack down, Antuan grabbed Jack's wrist and broke the capsule against his skin. The slime inside of it let loose, allowing him to slip the glove off of Jack's hand. Before Jack realized what had happened,

Antuan was running away toward one of the electric orbs and laughing.

"Yes! Loser!" He shouted back to Jack.

Reaching the closest orb, Antuan grabbed it in his gloved hands and threw it as hard as he could into the sky. Behind Antuan, Jack yelled in anger, "You cheater!" Out of fury, and ignoring the warning about the danger of the orbs, he snatched the first one he could reach. Excruciating pain consumed every part of his skin where the orb touched. With a desperate scream, Jack launched it up into the air, but he wasn't quick enough.

Antuan's orb was the first to explode, filling the sky with his wish for Bella's love. The gigantic shape of a heart burst into the blue sky. Jack's exploded but a second later sending a vibrant arrow piercing through the center of the shining heart and dashing Antuan's expectations. A gasp spread through the crowd followed with concerned whispers of "It's a curse!"

"What the heck?!" Antuan gasped glaring at Jack. "I swear you'll pay for this!"

But Antuan held his head high with pride and raised his hands triumphantly into the air, pretending not to care about his rival's antics. Only Jack saw the deep dismay hidden beneath his mask of self-importance.

As the fireworks disappeared, Grinage stood at the podium and raised his hand for silence. The audience grew still once again, but the excitement was palpable.

"Thank you, everyone, for joining us today for this great competition! You have all proven yourselves valuable participants!" Grinage turned to Sebastian and signaled the start of the victory ceremony.

"Carry on, Sebastian."

Sebastian stepped onto the podium and announced with a low powerful voice, "Now it's the time for the victory ceremony!" With a flick of his wrist, he made a black box appear instantly beside him on the stage. The king then used his powers to deliver the box into his general's hands, and Sebastian carried it to Isabella.

"Your Highness, please do the honors of displaying the winning trophy!"

Bella opened the box and her eyes went wide. Inside was a beautiful blue-crystal rabbit. She reached in to pick it up, and it sprang to life in her hands. Bella laughed with delight at the furry creature.

Sebastian called Antuan forth and gave him a bow and arrow. "Son, use this weapon wisely," he hissed at Antuan.

Turning back to address the crowd, he said, "Antuan will shoot an arrow at this blue rabbit. If he hits it, the animal will become a crystal decoration as he was before. If he misses the rabbit, it will stay alive and run free."

Everyone was cheering as Bella raised the rabbit high and kissed it for good luck. "Run like the wind," she gently whispered into the rabbit's ear, willing it to escape. She set the frightened animal down, and it took off, running as fast as it could as it maneuvered from side to side.

But Antuan was known for his marksmanship.

He took aim at the rabbit, following its movements before letting his arrow fly. Just as he let loose his arrow, Kace flung Bella's long scarf into Antuan's face with a surge of magic. The arrow went wild, missing the rabbit just as it disappeared into the tree line. Antuan scowled at his missed chance, but Bella cheered and clapped loudly.

Grinage frowned at Antuan's blunder, but he stood to make his announcement anyway. He walked toward the pedestal, taking Bella's hand to lead her beside him. With no warning, Bella went limp and fainted to the floor. The royal doctor rushed out to her side. From above the murmur of the crowd a woman's voice rang out, its tone dark and alarming.

"It's an omen," she cried.

Grinage looked at the spectators; they were all on their feet, chanting in unison, "Omen, omen, omen". He felt a strange chill run up and down his spine, warning him of some vague doom. He raised his arms to silence them.

"Nonsense," he shouted in anger. "And I will punish any who dare say otherwise!" He then declared the ceremony concluded and marched off leaving Bella to her attendants.

Change was coming.

Acknowledgement

My most heartfelt gratitude goes to my husband, twin daughters, and my son. I also want to thank all my dear friends and Rebecca Martinez, an extraordinary editor.

ABOUT THE AUTHOR

Margarita Kouznetsova, the mother of three, was born in 1974 in Siberia but grew up in an exclusive place called "Star City "where the astronauts lived and were trained. Everything about that place was magical; carefully defined lawns with fountains and colorful streetlights that casted off shapes of galaxies.
In 1998 she moved to the United States with her husband and son, and in September 2009 Margarita had a vivid idea of her book The Lost Twins of Zilonia.
She wrote the concept of it overnight, and it took her almost five years to complete the manuscript. During that time Margarita found out that she was expecting twin girls, which added a lot of new twists to the novel.

www.ingramcontent.com/pod-product-compliance
Lightning Source LLC
Chambersburg PA
CBHW071301170626
46809CB00001B/307